I0708664

A GLIMPSE OF THE NUMINOUS

Jeff Gardiner

A Glimpse of the Numinous
Publication Date: January 2012

Copyright Jeff Gardiner 2012.

Cover Art copyright David Rix 2012

ISBN: 978-1-908125-11-8

www.eibonvalepress.co.uk

<u>Acknowledgements</u>

A Glimpse of the Numinous – Fusing Horizons 4, 2004

351073 – 'The Elastic Book of Numbers', 2005. Elastic Press.

Writer's Block – Focus 47, 2005.

The Curious – 'New Wave of Speculative Fiction', 2005, Crowswing Books

More Sinned Against… – Writer's Muse serialised in 2006

Phobophilia – 'Subtle Edens: Elastic Book of Slipstream', Elastic Press, 2008

Bred In the Bone – Twisted Tongue 12, 2008

Dionysus – Estronomicon, 2009

Heartwood – Wicked Jungle, 2010

Past Away – 'Darkest Secrets', Static Movement 2010

Gull Power – Raphael's Village, 2010

In memory of my friend Roger Bastable.

"... that 'wholly other', whose profundities, impenetrable
to any concept, can yet be grasped in the numinous self-
feeling by one who has experience of the deeper life."

-Rudolf Otto, *The Idea of the Holy*

CONTENTS:

A GLIMPSE OF THE NUMINOUS

"We haven't made love for over a year now. Then one day a few weeks ago I was quite shocked when Helen began to masturbate in bed beside me in the early hours of the morning. She's never done that in all our married life. I have to admit, our sex life had never been up to much – it's not something that's ever really bothered us before. But the first time this happened, her moaning woke me and I thought she was having nightmares but when I tried to shake her she pushed me away. In the darkness I could hear and feel her reaching climaxes of ecstasy that she had certainly never experienced with me."

Dan paused for a while and would not catch my eye, for which I was grateful, as I wasn't sure I really wanted to hear this, but it was too late to stop him now.

"Initially I found it quite exciting feeling her spasms of pleasure that shook the whole bed. We never spoke about it, which added to the secretive thrill of it all. I felt like a grubby voyeur – and loved it." Dan drew another deep inhalation from his cigarette and let the smoke fall wispily from his nostrils. "I'm sorry if this is grossing you out, but I want you to understand everything that has happened." I nodded quickly and gestured for him to continue.

"Then I mentioned it to her and she stared at me like I was mental. She didn't know that she was doing it. I know that sounds stupid, but I wondered at first if she'd been hypnotised or something. Ever since her mum died she's got interested in spiritualist stuff … you know, that sort of bollocks you're into …"

"I'm not into that stuff," I protested with indignation. "I have a degree in Psychology and I like reading fantasy literature…"

"Exactly. All that wanky, new age, supernatural bullshit. That's what I mean…"

"Well, if you're just going to insult me then I'm off. I'll see myself out."

"No, no! Look, I'm sorry, I didn't mean that. Things have been weird recently and I really need a friend right now."

That was the funniest thing of all. He considered me his best friend, but I hardly knew the guy – even though he was my brother. To be honest, I didn't even like him and we had very little in common. We never had. He was a science teacher, but he didn't even read science fiction because it wasn't realistic and he would condemn great films like 'Blade Runner' or 'The Matrix' because of their lapses in logic or the implausible scientific veracity. When I spoke of imagination and exhilaration he would stare at me blankly. He really was one of those anally retentive types who cling to trivial facts and unswerving logic, never making that leap of faith that real scientists have to when developing new theories.

Now I felt sorry for him, although I had no idea how I could help him, and was worried what he was going to ask me to do. Intrigued by what he was going to tell me next, I agreed to stay and he fetched another couple of beers.

"This happened every single night for two weeks and it really turned me on. You know, I had to go and satisfy myself, if you get what I mean." I grimaced at this unnecessary information and resumed my listening expression.

"In fact, sex has always been rubbish between us, so we gave up a while ago and it's never been much of an issue."

"Perhaps you've just drifted apart. Have you considered a trial separation?"

"But I love her. I want us to stay together."

"Do you think she's having an affair?" I suggested insensitively.

"Maybe, I'm not sure it's that simple." He took a gulp of beer and I kept quiet as he clearly meant to continue. Anyway, he had me hooked.

"Don't laugh at what I'm about to tell you, but I'm just going to say it as I saw it.

"You know what I was saying about Helen's … um … night-time activities? Well, it got really spooky – to be honest I got shit-scared. One night last week I was woken again by her shuddering and heavy breathing and I turned to watch her slowly writhing. I could just make her out silhouetted in the gloom. As I lay there watching I felt something odd rub against my leg. It was rough and cold. Just fleetingly it touched me; it felt gnarled and bristly. I remember wondering what the hell it was." After a pause as he finished his beer, visibly shaken at the memory "I could only think that she'd scratched me with her toenails and that I imagined the rest – probably sleep deprivation. But it got worse."

I finished my beer and shifted to a more comfortable position.

"The next night I couldn't sleep, and was waiting for her to go through the routine again. It began with small moans and eventually her whole body shivered and then rocked before becoming more violent until the throes of her orgasm took over her entire body. By then my eyes had got used to the darkness and I could watch the changing shapes of her rippling under the duvet. As I watched her closely, starting to touch myself, I saw something that filled me with horror. Both her hands were lying on the pillow near her face as her short breaths signalled the closeness of her orgasm. Between her legs a shape was moving. Something was under there. Flinging the bedclothes from me I leapt up and slapped the light switch on. Helen looked up at me dazed, as if just woken from a deep sleep, with concern in her eyes. Her nightdress was pulled up to her neck and she wore no underwear. I saw a shadow shuffle off the end of the bed. I saw it! It was small and squat; inhuman. By then I was shouting and she was crying. Helen thought I'd gone crazy as I looked under the bed, in the wardrobe – everywhere. Then I grabbed hold of her by the throat and demanded to know the truth. Still she pleaded ignorance until I realised that I was genuinely hurting her. I apologised and we embraced with the first sign of affection between us for ages.

"After that it stopped. She slept right through for a couple of nights and I had hoped that was the end of it. You know, I'm starting to worry about my own sanity."

There followed a long pause during which I wondered why, exactly, he had called me. As I looked more closely at him it occurred to me that maybe he was slightly mad. He had always been a bit tense and overwrought; one of those people who could never quite relax and be at ease with the world. Perhaps that and the sheer frustration of his strange marriage have led to something of a breakdown. It seemed he interpreted my expression, as he answered my silent question.

"Since then, one more thing has happened. I came back from work yesterday and I found the living room all smashed up as if we'd had intruders. But there was no sign of a break in."

"Did you call the police?"

"No. I didn't want to."

"You think Helen did it?"

"She was asleep in bed, oblivious to everything – or so she claimed. But she had bruises on her face and arms."

"God, she needs to see a doctor – a psychiatrist."

"Yes, I know, but there's a problem with that. She won't let me."

"I think you need to stand up to her, Dan." I never thought I'd have to say that as he was always by far the most dominant one in their marriage.

"Yes, but what if they think I beat her? I don't know what I'm supposed to do, now. If she accuses me of hitting her I'll lose my job and go to jail."

For a fleeting second I wondered if he was lying and that he had hit her. Was there a dark side to my brother? These worries were allayed when I saw the fear in his eyes quickly transform into desperation.

"You have to help me. Please say you will. There's no one else I can turn to. And what's more, Helen knows and trusts you."

It was pity for my brother that most overwhelmed me and I consented to helping him. I suppose the family bond is a powerful one, even if I found him annoying and, at times, more than tedious. Dan's plan was for me to take Helen to my house in the belief that a change of scenery would do her good – or in Dan's words "maybe even stop this nonsense". In his mind he was hoping that I could psychoanalyse her and diagnose this crazy behaviour. I tried to explain to him that my expertise was in coaching and motivating top sports stars and athletes, but he wouldn't have it. For him psychology was pagan mumbo-jumbo – pseudo-science for hippies – but helpful for the diagnosis of his insane wife. I kept my feelings quiet as I was doing this more for her than for him and the whole thing was intriguing me no end.

What occurred to me was that Dan was the one who had seen a mysterious shadow – not Helen. All she could be accused of so far was sexual frustration and anger. If they're signs of lunacy then put me down for a lobotomy.

She didn't complain when we explained what was going to happen and got willingly into my car. My house was about an hour's drive away through the Sussex countryside. Even though I was a confirmed bachelor, who preferred short affairs to long-term commitment, I did live in an overly substantial detached house, built to look like a villa and that backed on to a field that swept up to the South Downs. It was an ideal location for us to walk and talk together and spend the weekend sorting out my brother's marriage.

It has to be said that I'm not a good psychologist, but I still have some limited understanding of clinical depression and schizophrenia. Most of my recent reading, however, had been those tacky NLP 'help-yourself' guides full of soundbites and ersatz philosophy. Not because I agreed with them, but because I was lazy and it was easy to impress people by learning little nuggets of knowledge. I know this makes me a hypocrite because that's exactly what annoys me about my brother.

To my great surprise I really enjoyed our initial walks and chats and it was a pleasure to get to know my sister-in-law, which I had never actually done because I rarely saw Dan and I'd never seen her on her own before. At first she was reticent, but my skill at flattery turned that to mere coyness, until she responded to my opening up to her about some of my own insecurities and personal feelings. This led to her confiding in me her growing interest in pantheism, which interested me, but her ideas were never made explicit. However, what I saw on her second night here I certainly had not been expecting.

A loud crash woke me up and I ran downstairs bleary-eyed, expecting to find Helen smashing up my front room, as she had her own, but instead I found my back door wide open and saw that a tall parlour palm had been knocked over; its vase had smashed into shards spilling earth and roots over my expensive carpet. It wasn't necessary to check her room, as it was obvious that this wasn't the work of intruders. Luckily I could see her figure just disappearing through the hedge at the bottom of my garden. I grabbed a long coat and followed her. How the bloody hell was I supposed to explain to Dan what I saw and experienced next?

Passing through the same gap in the hedge I found myself in the familiar lea that led to the mystical downs. Dark, rising slopes ahead of me met the majestic sky flecked with stars. Night-time has its own smell and I inhaled heavily. In the distance I heard the distinctive 'coo-ick' of a nightjar, no doubt hunting for moths in mid-flight. Sheep often wandered through here and I hoped that I wouldn't stumble upon any now. The ground was uneven and difficult to negotiate in the moonlight, so I expected to catch up with Helen quite quickly. However, I was surprised to see that she had already reached the summit and was stood upon a rock, silhouetted in the gloaming. I broke into a trot and as I neared her, she seemed unaware of my presence. In the half-light her form was clearly naked and more shapely than I had ever noticed before. Helen had never previously struck me as attractive. This made me stop in my tracks about ten metres behind her. I'm ashamed to admit that my first impulse was sexually motivated. This sounds crass when I say it, but I felt an overwhelming urge, like a sexual frisson. Nothing crude, like a sudden hard-on; this was a feeling I had never had before. A sound entered my consciousness, but I wasn't sure if I was hearing it or whether it was vibrating right inside me. It was a breathy whistle or perhaps a sigh that echoed within my head and loins, and even though I could not follow the direction from whence it came, I just knew that it was connected with this woman ahead of me. Nothing made any logical sense any more, but it was as if a natural instinct within me had taken over, offering me an insight into some new experience.

Frozen to the ground as I was, I kept my gaze upon Helen whose naked outline had me entranced. She slowly turned and I could not help but gasp as I beheld her imposing loveliness. It was her, but not her; as if she had taken on a different shape, but retained the essence of herself. Moonbeams danced playfully upon her breasts and shadows flowed over her like loving caresses as she moved towards me. What I could not understand was how she moved. I couldn't see her feet move and yet she was travelling closer to me. It appeared that she didn't so much walk as hover or slide.

And then she touched me. Oh God, what sensations shot through me. Like someone imparting the truth behind life's complex enigmas. So much more than a paltry orgasm: this shook creation's foundations – made my body and soul quake in unison. Before me stood my brother's wife and I wanted nothing more than to touch her new-found perfection and to kiss every inch of her, as if to do so would set my spirit on fire and let me melt into the wondrous universe. If to embrace her was to die, then death held no fear for me.

I allowed my trembling hand to slowly reach out as my fingers wrapped urgently about her softness, clasping her with a desire to absorb her deep within me. That embrace hurled us to another place and time – a place beyond time. Her smells and textures were familiar and yet I had hardly touched the woman before that moment. My being was filled with what I can only describe as a savage tenderness. I needed to destroy and then create: to hunt and worship.

Her eyes glistened with a distant, lustrous pain: a longing, a loneliness. She slipped her hands under my coat to let her fingertips tease and tantalize me to distraction. Our bodies touched and it felt like they were somehow connected then dissolving into each other. For a fraction of a second we tasted eternity as we danced together like entwining serpents.

It was then that I ripped her from me, reeling back in a demented panic as ethereal visions exploded in my mind. Helen stumbled backwards and I finaly saw what she had become. Her legs had fused together and seemed to have lengthened, tapering to a point and then curling up behind her. A smooth belly gradated imperceptibly into a scaly skin. From her waist up she was still human and her head was one of sublime beauty, now with long, black, alluring hair, which before had been short and greying. Was she some sort of a shape-shifter in mid-transformation? I swear that her lower body had become that of a serpent or at least it flickered between snake and human as if she was some magical, malleable spirit showing me two sides of her very being.

A hiss and snarl behind me forced me to spring round and I saw squat shapes leap about, scuttling off into a nearby copse. Eyes were watching me from all around. I felt a presence lingering: was aware of it rather than saw it. The low movements about me were too deft and fleeting for me to capture the essence of any definite shape or form. I knew these were not sheep, but what they actually were was beyond my understanding.

The first jostle alarmed me, but then I felt myself being bashed and bombarded as these brutish creatures began to hurl themselves at me. Each one was a different size and shape and as each one fell to the ground, would either vanish or change its form before hurtling away to renew its attack. This grim assault was also launched with unworldly grunts and screeches – new sounds to these ears.

But something else very strange was also happening to me, which has taken me a long time to come to terms with. It is still something I do not fully understand, but something I will spend the rest of my life attempting to invoke or summon back. With each beating I received I became aware of an animal instinct within me; what I can only call a primal consciousness that awoke a latent presence from somewhere deep inside my very soul. An anger began to seethe and rise like bile, shaking my innards and flowing through my blood. I felt a desperate desire to kick out, but not like a human. This is the strange thing. I wanted to turn around and kick out at them from behind with what I imagined were hooves at the end of my powerful legs. Then the urge to gallop took over, to find others like me and run with them – to stampede and lose control and allow ourselves to feel each other's anger and ecstasy. Only then would the loneliness disappear and in unity with nature would we laugh and canter and skip with the freedom as children of the universe – together.

I did run. I must have done, because when I came back to earthly consciousness I was lying on the cold, hard stones of the beach with the incoming tide lapping at my feet. Frozen and shaken with a giddiness over the previous night's events, I became concerned for the whereabouts of Helen. What in God's name had happened? What would Dan have to say? Being still early in the morning there was nobody around, just inquisitive and noisy gulls hoping I might be a fresh carcass for them to scavenge. My entire body ached and my neck clicked and snapped as I twisted my head round. Clad only in boxer shorts, I jogged as well as I could back to my home and found the back door still open. I called for Helen but there was no sign that she had even returned so I lay down wondering in my confused state what would be the best thing to do.

"I'm coming over to see you – now." It was Dan. When the phone rang two days later I panicked and wasn't going to answer it, but then lifted the receiver expecting the police. Dan had put the phone down straight after his terse announcement and didn't give me a chance to ask him if he'd seen Helen or if she was okay. I had sequestered myself in bed for nearly forty hours, waiting for something to happen.

When the bell rang I opened the door furtively. There was Dan, his eyes narrowed over his red cheeks. He barged the door with his shoulders and shoved me onto the floor. Before I could react he had his knee pressing heavily into my groin.

"You bastard," he growled. "I trusted you."

Had something else happened that night? What was it? Was Helen dead? Had I killed her in that frenzy of madness?

"Dan. Please. What the fuck is going on?"

Ignoring my pleas, he pounded a fist into my face. The searing pain made me howl and trip backwards. Then he clamped his hands around my neck to throttle me. His thumbs squeezed down on my adam's apple and I gasped for air. Before he could rip right through my throat I heaved with all my might and threw him against the wall. His head jolted back and I heard the thud as his skull hit the concrete. I was shocked with my brute strength. With such ease I had actually lifted him bodily and flung him aside. I tended to him immediately and carried him to my favourite chair. Glad to see his eyelids flutter, I poured out a large scotch to offer him when he finally came round. Whilst I waited I drank one myself.

He seemed grateful for the whisky and had visibly calmed down, offering no further threat to me. His blood-shot eyes still looked at me with some vehemence. This time I got in first.

"What the hell is going on, Dan? What is it you think I've done? Helen disappeared – I swear."

With his head tilted slightly he gave me a sideways and inquisitive look.

"Just answer me one question. Did you screw my wife?"

"No, I swear to you, I wouldn't do that." How could I explain to him what had happened, when I wasn't sure myself?

"Then what have you done to her?"

"What're you on about?"

Dan gulped down the rest of his whisky and wiped his mouth with his sleeve.

"It's Helen. She came back last night. She's changed and she's got new ideas that are just not her speaking. So I wondered where she'd got them from."

"Whoa, mate. I've got no idea what you're talking about. So Helen's okay then? Well, thank God for that."

"She wants new rules and parameters for our marriage." He held out his glass for a top up. "Our marriage isn't satisfying her and she wants us to have a more free and open relationship."

"What does that mean?"

"Don't be so naïve. She wants to be able to shag other blokes."

"Not necessarily…"

"I was just wondering if you had planted these shitty ideas in her brain whilst you were busily psychoanalysing my wife?"

"That's bloody ridiculous. I'm not some hypnotist who can force people to do what I want. If she's got this idea it must stem from somewhere in her own repressed, unconscious mind."

"I'm not going to change things just for her convenience."

"Do you think she's rejecting you, then? Does she want to leave you?"

"Not exactly. In fact she seemed very interested in me, you know, sexually."

"Well, that's good, isn't it?"

"She came over a bit desperate, to tell the truth. She demanded sex from me there and then."

"Blimey."

"There's me worried about her health and she comes back wanting rampant sex."

"Excellent. You did tell me yourself that it had been a long time."

"Yeah, but it didn't feel right. She seemed kind of obsessed and more experienced than she had been before."

"Well, one of you had to take the lead, I guess."

"I got scared." His tone was lost and pathetic, and I'm afraid I laughed but he wasn't impressed with my response. He shot me a scowl.

"Sorry, Dan, but isn't that every man's dream? To marry a nymphomaniac? Let her take the lead, then. You might enjoy yourself."

"So you'd know would you?"

I stopped laughing. So he still suspected me.

"Look, I'm sorry, but you're wrong about us."

Dan continued with his explanation as if I had said nothing. "I didn't recognise her. This wasn't the woman I married."

"What, because you can't control her any more?"

"Excuse me?"

"You need to give her some slack. Let her do her thing. There's more to her than you think. She's not just a little obedient housewife with no thoughts of her own." I stared at him incredulously as if suddenly enlightened and I saw him with new eyes. "You truly have no idea who she really is, do you? And you never will understand who she is, because you have absolutely no idea who you are yourself."

"Oh, I know who she is. She's my wife – or she was. Something has happened to her and it's sent her crazy. She insane – I dunno – schizophrenic. Whatever it is she's not normal."

"Normal? What the hell is normal?" I raised my voice, infuriated by his short-sightedness.

"Don't give me your twisted bullshit philosophy. We live in the real world and you need to realise it. Normal is what the world agrees upon. It's to do with being civilised and following reason. It's all we have."

How do you begin to explain something to someone who can't use the senses he was given? Because I didn't answer his eyes lit up in victory and he smiled smugly to himself. For him logic had won the debate. Then just like all bad winners, he couldn't leave it there, but had to compound his so-called triumph further.

"Something happened between you two and I want to know what it was." His face had a new expression of determination that made me grin.

"You'll never understand what happened, – mainly because it doesn't fit into your precious science curriculum."

"Yeah? Well you live in a dreamworld. You never made the break as a child from fairy tales. There comes a time in your life when you have to grow up and understand that the real world is very different from your fantasies."

"Don't patronise me. If I live in a dreamworld, then you live in a sad and squalid little prison cell. Not only is your life narrow and limited but you're paid by the state to indoctrinate children with your trivial views." That silenced him. "You've never really lived, that's your problem. Your wife comes back to you and because she's a bit different you reject her and call her mad. You're the one who's insane, Dan." I couldn't stop now – I was on a roll. "Helen finally found out who she is. What you don't see is that life is more than three-dimensional. Logic is bollocks. Life is chaotic, Dan. Nature is unpredictable – that's the world we live in, not one that abides by a neat set of rules. Cause and effect? Scientific laws and principals? All of it's absolute bollocks." Now it was my turn to pause for effect, before going in for the kill.

"There is life beyond what's material – call it what you like – spirit, soul, supernatural, magic, emotions, the id. Body and soul are connected to something greater, deeper than science. Call it God, or Nature, or the Cosmic Universe – whatever – it doesn't matter. Some people discover something within themselves and that moment is like a religious experience as they tap into something …" I searched for the appropriate term, "… numinous." I let him take it all in, which he was struggling to do judging by his bemused expression.

"Helen had a weird experience out on the downs. I'm not exactly sure what happened, but I saw it. She became something … different – but I believe that somehow what she became is the real her."

"Now you're the one talking bollocks What you mean is she's schizophrenic and in your own deluded world you think you saw something because you wanted to. Then again, you might be making all this up just to cover up for what really happened."

"I knew you'd be like this," I sighed with frustration. "She has experienced something amazing and you're not willing to open your mind to it." I shook my head in exasperation.

"Maybe you both deserve each other."

"Look forget it, huh? You're not listening to me."

"Yeah, because you're lying. You fucked my wife and fed her lies to turn her away from me. You're pathetic. You're not my brother and I hope I never see you or her again." And he swept out, slamming the door behind him. All I could feel for him was pity – and that didn't last long.

His wishes came true. I have no idea where Helen went, and I heard through a cousin that Dan is now a Deputy Head in the Midlands.

I've tried to think through what exactly did happen that night. I have come to realise that my feelings towards whatever Helen had become were more than just sexual urges – it was more profound in an odd way. I believe what I experienced was some sort of self-discovery and just like Helen, I too had had this glimpse of the numinous. I sometimes wish I had abandoned my ego completely and allowed myself to taste the ecstasy offered by my union with that other being. And now I swear to myself that I will do everything I can to recreate that moment and let myself fall once more into that beautiful, frightening chasm of primal consciousness. Hopefully, there I will discover who or what I truly am.

The day my daughter was born was both the worst and best day of my life, although at the time I only felt the devastation. My wife, Fran, had been ill for some years and we had assumed that we were not to be blessed with children. So when she gleefully told me one night after parish council that she thought she might be pregnant I whispered a prayer as she stepped into the bathroom to try the home test. She had been good enough to wait patiently for me, wondering when my parishioners would finally release me for the night. They did frequently forget that I also have a home and a wife who deserves my time and attention.

The good Lord answered our prayer and we made an appointment with our doctor who did very little except congratulate us and tell Fran what she couldn't eat. Of course we saw the midwife, had the scans and did all the classes as a couple. I was determined to be a dedicated father and share all things equally. Fran also worked full-time and her salary was worth more than twice mine.

On the fateful day it was clear that things were wrong from the beginning. I was hustled out of the way and nobody would answer my frantic questions, including God, as it seemed at the time. So I didn't see the birth as it all happened behind closed doors. They sent two smartly dressed manager-types to tell me the shocking news. Fran had not survived, but I had a baby girl. My brother and sister-in-law were with me at the time, hugging and holding me as I shook and sobbed; but it seemed like I was alone in a void. Only my faith kept me sane.

It was many hours before I could bring myself to look at the baby. Our baby. My baby. The hospital decided to keep her in for a few days under observation and I was advised to go home and rest. I did as I was told. My team Rector came round to pray with me and told me he would look after things at my church for the next few weeks whilst I sorted things out. I was extremely grateful to him and to the overwhelming support I received from the many friends in my wonderful congregation. Food was brought round as well as flowers and cards with loving messages of support and kindness.

My neighbour took me back to hospital the next day to meet my daughter. When I saw her I broke down, crying with more passion than I had felt for over twenty years. The tears were for the loss of Fran and the wasted dreams; but also for the joy of seeing such a delicate and vulnerable creature squirming and holding out her hands in need of warmth and security. She had to be my priority now.

Of course, Fran and I had discussed names, but for some reason they didn't seem appropriate any more. One part of me thought I should choose Fran's favourite, which was Leanne, but a voice in me told me it wasn't right. When I looked at her little face and blinking eyes, they weren't the eyes of a Leanne. I wondered if I should call her Fran, but it's important for a child to be an individual and not a copy of her parents.

The first night that I took my precious baby home, I refused all offers of help and company, except for the midwife visitors, and lay with her on my bed, gazing lovingly at her minute perfection. She screamed and made a mess, but who cares? She was mine: a gift from God to prove that all is not bad in the world. I had expected myself to hate God for not saving my wife. But instead I thanked Him for this little miracle.

As I lay on the bed next to the strangely gurgling creature next to me, I wondered again about a name. We had bought books that listed thousands, but none sounded completely suitable. It was as I lay there, my head twisted towards her leg which stretched up awkwardly and hovered before my eyes, that I saw she still wore the hospital identity tag on her little ankle. I stared at it and was stunned to see that it had written on it, 'ELOISE'. And it was so perfect. My little Eloise. It was pretty and elegant. But why on earth was it already written on her band? Who had named her? I gently took hold of it and stared hard for a few minutes. The name Eloise stood out but then the letters following it were meaningless symbols. And then I chuckled at my stupidity, having to stop myself from choking. What an idiot. I carefully sat up and read the it other way up. It was just a list of numbers printed out in computerised digits and the last six numbers were 351073, which upside down looked exactly like ELOISE.

I kissed Eloise and put her into her crib, ready to sleep for a few hours until her next feed.

As she grew up Eloise took great delight in the story of her naming and was already telling people how it was fate: a message from above. When she looked it up she found that Eloise meant 'noble one', which was very appropriate, for she grew into a very beautiful and confident young lady. She took to signing herself as 351073, which confused people, but was always a good conversation starter. When she found she could program her name into a calculator, it was the beginning of a whole language created by her and her best friends. In her teens she acquired a mobile and started sending and receiving rude and silly messages by text, turning the phone upside down to read them. I didn't think to stop her. With the tragedy at the beginning of her life the least I could do was allow my Eloise to have some fun.

Whilst my faith is of great importance to me I had resolved from the very beginning never to force my beliefs on Eloise. I consider myself a liberal preacher, who teaches tolerance and compassion, rather than fire and brimstone. Being shaky on eschatological theology, I preferred to base sermons on the beatitudes of Christ that encouraged love and peace amongst our fellow men. Of course I wanted Eloise to continue coming to church and build up her own independent Christian faith, but alas, like so many modern young people she soon became bored and disillusioned and couldn't wait to explore more exciting and fulfilling experiences. The silly thing is I understood how she felt and had been expecting it when she finally came to me and asked if she could go round to her friend's one Sunday morning. I smiled and nodded and she never stepped foot inside a church again.

I guessed that she was meeting boys and probably sleeping with them. But I preferred not to know. One time she came home drunk and I tried to act casual when she came down the next morning with a hangover, but my laughter was hollow.

I blame myself for her active and continuing interest in numerology. It stemmed from my discovery of her name and she convinced herself that her name was pre-ordained; somehow given to her by providence. She discovered the arcane writings of Pythagoras who proclaimed that you could discover the essence of any person by working out their root number. From these mysterious figures, secrets of great spiritual significance could be identified concerning one's future and personality.

Eloise would try to explain things to me with immense patience.

"The basic principals of the cosmos can be expressed through numbers…"

"That's where you're losing me, darling. What do you mean by 'basic principals of the cosmos'?"

"I mean that mathematics can help us gain a greater knowledge of the metaphysical world."

"Oh, really? Blimey and I hated maths when I was younger."

"Don't take the mick, Dad. I don't laugh at your beliefs." She didn't like it when I was flippant about the things she took seriously. I didn't want her to give up or get defensive.

"No, you're right, I'm sorry. I think I'm just being a bit thick. Do go on."

Then Eloise would blind me with complex aphorisms that were either meaningless mumbo-jumbo or mind-bending paradoxes. Some of her proverbs made good sense though.

"There is no absolute truth: only the truth of the Absolute," she enigmatically confided to me one day. As I thought about it I realised that we might have common ground.

"I think I can happily say I agree with you on that one," I responded triumphantly. Obviously our definitions of who or what the 'Absolute' might be, would probably differ greatly. So I left it there. She would still hug me and cuddle up with me on the sofa even at the age of eighteen. Eloise was a very affectionate and thoughtful daughter.

Then she would leave me little notes in unexpected places: the fridge, my underwear drawer, or even clipped to my latest sermon.

"The secrets of nature will guide humanity to a harmonious destiny," it would say. Or "Man is not body. The heart, the spirit is man – Paracelsus." Now I had no quibble with these little soundbites. I wasn't too sure what was meant by 'secrets of nature' – as long as she wasn't dabbling in witchcraft. And Paracelsus may not be my hero, but I was glad that Eloise appreciated that life is also spiritual. I certainly believe it – being a vicar.

The part I had a problem understanding was when she seemed obsessed with numbers. She frequently quoted Pythagoras: "Every man has been made by God in order to acquire knowledge and contemplate". This sounded wrong to me – far too Gnostic for my liking. Surely love and peace are more important than knowledge.

Above her bed Eloise had made a huge colourful poster with a collage of pictures of herself with family and friends, including two with me. These photographs framed a carefully lettered quotation from her favourite Greek that said, "All things can be expressed in numerical terms because all things are ultimately reducible to numbers". Then beneath it in a kaleidoscope of colours was her own numerical name: 351073. That one left me cold. I tried to explain to her that she was so much more than just that number, but she merely laughed and said with a twinkle, "Well, you can always shorten my name to 31773." It took me a while to work that one out.

Her interest in occult writing didn't stop there, though. Eloise found a fascination in Kabbalism, alchemy, druidry and any mystical system that delighted in number, calendars, cycles or secret alphabets. Her conversation quickly turned to concepts of 'astral projection' or 'transpersonal consciousness', whatever the heck that is. When she tried to explain to me the Tree of Life from the Kabbalah, supposedly a logical map with many levels that guide the adept into a so-called 'Divine Union', I stared at its eleven circles and twenty-two connecting pillars and could make little sense of its context or meaning.

Eloise saw me shaking my head and squinting.

"You see, men have wisdom, but women have understanding." She smiled as if this explained all my doubts and frustrations.

It was from then that things started getting really strange.

Eventually, she left home and travelled. I got e-mails from New Zealand, Israel, Thailand and Greece all from username 351073. She apologised for leaving me and hoped I didn't miss her too much. But I missed her terribly. I had moved to a new parish and even become Rector but life without Eloise was empty and too quiet for my liking. I missed the cut and thrust of debate and harmless conflict that always occurred between us. It's fair to say that Eloise challenged me to think for myself, rather than just rely on what I had been socialised into believing. I don't mean I lost my faith or felt any great desire to become a druid or join the Freemasons or anything, I was just aware that she helped me to think for myself – which has got to be a good thing. Even Christianity, which has a strict doctrine, scripture and creed, allows the individual to think out of the box on occasions. Or at least, in the Church of England it does.

Some of her messages became encoded and unreadable as she began to develop her own system of employing numbers and symbols to represent objects and people. I don't just mean like this lazy way of writing text messages by missing out vowels and using '4' instead of 'for' or where your friend is your 'best m8'. She had contrived a complex system of numbers that became letters when written slightly differently then turned upside down. But I refused to decipher these daft cryptographs. Sending them back to her I demanded that she communicated using Standard English. I didn't hear from her again for several months.

When I did eventually receive a message from her she was in Egypt and she sent me a reading of my 'Life Path Number', which I'd never heard of before, but is apparently 6. According to this my inner being is characterised by feelings of responsibility, protection and balance, whilst I am ostensibly community-oriented. Well, it seemed accurate enough although I had no idea how much she had just made up from her knowledge of me. I took it as a sign that I was forgiven. But then she said she was concerned about my 'Existential Emanation Integer' that pointed to some kind of tragedy, but would also lead to personal awareness and self-knowledge, helping me ultimately to contribute to the universal order. Of course I scoffed, as I do when I read in my stars that I will meet somebody. When don't you?

Her next e-mail announced that she was coming home at the end of the month and I wept with joy. I hadn't seen her for four years.

The changes were obvious. She had cut her hair short and was unnecessarily using dark eye make-up. And then I saw Eloise's tattoo. It was a sunny day and we were in the garden playing cricket – something we had done together since she was about three. She turned and bent down to pick up the ball when I saw a flash of something blue printed on the small of her back. My first reaction was to wonder how painful it had been as that part is so close to the pelvic bone. Her smile disappeared when I asked her about it.

"Is it a skull and crossbones? Or maybe 'I love Dad'?" I smiled pointing to the side of her hip.

"Neither, although it's true that I love you."

Little moments like that warm parents' hearts.

After some convincing she showed me the design. It was a number – what else. 5151.

"Another cryptic message?" I asked narrowing my eyes profoundly. "Let's see. Five thousand one hundred and fifty-one … hmmm … five one five one. Nope. It's not a boy's phone number is it, or the name of a band?" We giggled together but she still wouldn't tell me. "You see, what confuses me is that it can be reduced down to, um, two fives are ten plus two is twelve, which is further reduced to three. A magic number?"

"Well, I'm impressed with your knowledge of simple numerology, Dad. Perhaps you're not a completely lost soul just yet." She stabbed me with her forefinger. "I may well love you, but it doesn't stop you being extremely dim. Watch, Mr. Thicky." She turned around, walked up to our apple tree and cartwheeled into a very neat handstand. 'ISIS' was emblazoned clearly upon her bare midriff. It was on her front and back, like she was a stick of seaside rock with the name running through her.

I did extensive research on Isis as Eloise wouldn't tell me the significance. I knew Isis was from Egyptian mythology, but I discovered that she was a supreme goddess with unlimited power; an Earth Mother who became associated with burial and resurrection. Most interestingly, she was considered the goddess of wisdom who initiates people into occult mysteries. I was led to the writings of Madame Blavatsky, but found them vacuous and artificial.

I had been wondering about the strange symbols on Eloise's bag: horns clasped round a circle. These were symbols of Isis – the circle was a solar disc. Eloise also had a bracelet with an ankh dangling as a charm. She did explain to me that the ankh was a symbol of the unity of body and soul.

Family and friends were glad to see her return, but some spoke to me behind her back and warned me of her 'satanic' tendencies. This made me angry. Okay, so she had gone a bit hippy and new age, but she believed in love and spirituality, albeit in a slightly unorthodox form. Some of my parishioners even dared to suggest that I should kick her out of the house, and it's likely that they thought I was a bad father and an even worse clergyman – one who couldn't even convert his own daughter. Nobody said it, but I knew that some doubted my faith and integrity.

We spent a wonderful few months together going on picnics and walks; to theme parks and cricket matches. Eloise spoilt me, and her company made me so happy and content. She didn't like to talk about herself much and when I mentioned anything mystical or numerical she went silent and rapidly changed the subject. The only time she responded was when I thanked her for the Life Path reading.

"It certainly described me."

"You've always been generous and you put others first." She hugged me and skipped off a little way before stopping to let me catch her up.

"Not in any way detrimental to you, I hope," I asked anxiously.

"Don't be silly, Dad. I always felt loved and cherished. You have no need to worry." She looked me in the eye as she spoke. "I've always felt needed and secure. That's the gift you gave me. You've allowed me to be independent – to think for myself. You have no idea what that means."

Eloise took my hand and we walked a long way in silence. My heart was on fire.

"It's because of you that I can do what I have done."

"What do you mean?"

At first she was silent, gathering her thoughts. "You must promise not to interrupt. Let me finish before you say anything." I nodded assent.

"My name was the first sign…"

I was about to speak but remembered my promise.

"… but then my first real awareness of my metaphysical destiny came when I calculated and read my own life numbers. I kept checking them and had them verified independently and I knew then that I couldn't escape my fate."

I was still fighting the urge to ask a million questions, but I kept it to a dumb, quizzical look.

"You see, whatever way it was done, I came out as 22." My blank face revealed my ignorance as to the significance of this. "22 is the master number. It denotes a visionary – a leader on this plane of existence. It endows the individual with an inner power. The number 22 is a sign of enlightenment and individuation."

"So what does that make you? Some sort of chosen one?" I was shocked by such an heretical idea. What would my dear congregation think of me now with my daughter claiming to be some kind of prophet or messiah?

"Do you believe in the concept of Immanence?"

"I believe that God's spirit is in all things, because he created everything."

"God is one way of understanding the divine. I believe that the divine is manifest in all things and that man is a microcosm of our spiritual universe. The purpose of life is to seek inner knowledge, contemplate its mysteries and follow the paths to the World of Emanation. Some people are put on this world with a higher knowledge and awareness of their Divine-Self. These leaders are ordained to guide others towards that same blissful and harmonious destiny."

"And that leader is you?" I said it calmly and casually.

"It began with my name and it was you who found my name. I have that to thank you for." But that was not what I wanted to hear. I should have got angry with her and told her to see sense. I didn't. Instead I stood there dumbstruck, watching my daughter lose all sense of reason.

She stepped forward with a serene look on her beautiful face and embraced me.

"I love you, Dad. I'll always love you. Please don't ever be angry with me."

It felt like goodbye. Why would she be saying goodbye? But stupidly I ignored the warnings in my head. And the next day she had gone.

I mourned her then. I raged and smashed up the things around me. I swore at people. Belongings were trashed and broken. People were too frightened to see me. Feeling my life was over I sank into a deep depression and could not continue with my ministry. Where was my so-called loving God now? I swore at him and cursed his name.

The bishop sensibly told my church that I was on long-term sick leave whilst he took responsibility for the everyday running, along with the parish wardens. They found a curate who agreed to take Sunday services for the next few months. Encouraged to seek counselling and help, I tried to pull myself out of my morose stupor. Where the hell was Eloise? How could I find her? She didn't answer her e-mails and she didn't carry a phone.

From that moment I was tortured by numbers cascading in my dreams, devouring all my thoughts. I saw significance in all figures and digits. My heart leapt when I got a new visa card and there in the middle of the long number on the front were six letters in exactly the right order: 351073. My first thought was that she was somehow contacting me, but then I wondered if it was, as she said, a mark of destiny. What if we were all subject to some cosmic fate – a pattern that had been set for eternity?

Other weird things began to happen. Or did they? Perhaps my mind was deluding me. Or maybe I was just seeing things for the first time that have always been around me. When I finally struggled out on my own, unshaved and watched warily by many familiar passers-by, my weekly shopping came to £51.51. What was the likelihood of that? Was Eloise, or someone else, playing a game with me?

I tried e-mailing and phoning anybody who might know her. When I called the police they asked on what grounds I considered her 'missing' and even though I tried my best to explain, they concluded that she was just a religious nut and advised me to contact some specialist service and counsellor. I had images of myself kidnapping and deprogramming her, but it was just wish fulfilment.

Eventually via search engines and a lot of good luck I discovered a website entitled '5151:ISIS'. Clicking on the hyperlink 'Isis Within' I found a long explanation of how numerology had been used to identify a master adept, called a 'human-divine'. This certain individual had discovered that she was an incarnation of Isis and that the Universal Spirit had chosen her to lead humanity into their rightful harmonious destiny, known as Bliss. I wondered at first if 'Bliss' was a drug reference and that Eloise had just got caught up with some kind of hippy, psychedelic malarkey.

I tried to contact Eloise through the website, but the only reply I got told me that I must visit Bliss. Nobody would give me any more information. After hours of surfing the web I was ready to give up for the night, when it struck me that I must think cryptically. How would Eloise refer to Bliss? Eventually, I found a new website called 55178. com and imagined in my head her voice calling me Mr. Thicky. I was shaking as I read the introductory page and I recognised her words and the familiar imagery of ankh, horns and disc. The references to the work of the 'human-divine', the reincarnation of Isis, amazed and stunned me. My own daughter was the leader of a cult. She had supposedly cured people and performed miracles, giving accurate readings of people's futures and considered a spiritual leader. The secrets were communicated through the arcane numbering that she had developed, connected with various ancient alphabets and Kabbalistic diagrams.

As Isis, Eloise seemed to believe that universal order would come about when she re-entered the underworld to be reunited with Osiris. She described herself as the most perfect microcosm: the key to the Macrocosm.

"My destiny," she wrote, and I could hear her voice saying the words, "is to leave this material world and find the next plane of existence from where I shall be able to help and guide those who have reached the sphere of spirituality and who desire a guide into the Blissful Realm of the Divine. I await you there."

My hand was shaking as if I knew what to expect next. I managed to move the curser, using the mouse, onto another link on a sidebar called 'Logging In'. Up came a small box that said 'Please Enter Existential Number'. Without thinking I typed in 351073, pressed return and waited.

At first the screen turned to static and I thought there was some kind of fault. But then a dim image became apparent – some kind of video clip. There before my eyes was my baby – my daughter, Eloise. When she spoke to me I felt my heart leap within my ribcage.

"Hello, Dad."

I responded as if she was in the room with me.

"Hello, my darling. How are you?"

But, of course, she didn't respond. She just kept speaking. It was a recording – but from when?

"Dad, I know you won't understand what I'm doing, but I don't want you to be angry or upset. I've found my true purpose in life – and how many people can say that much, huh? Just as you believe you followed your vocation into the church, I know that this is my harmonious destiny. Just as you believe your Jesus died for the salvation of mankind, so I believe that fate has created a path for me, which will benefit humanity. I couldn't tell you about it before because I knew you would try to talk me out of it. You understand about rituals – you have plenty in the church. Well, these universal rituals exist in cycles and it is time once more for Isis to return to the underworld."

To my initial horror the camera panned out to show her standing on a cliff edge. I didn't recognise the location. It was some kind of gorge or canyon. Then I was aware of my own faltering breath as I watched through tearful eyes.

"Death is not the end, Dad. I know you believe it. Let it strike no fear in you. Death can only bring peace and is a new step on a never-ending journey. Always look beyond and believe in the union of spirits."

I was weeping silently as I watched her signal to someone off camera. She turned back to the camera, which zoomed in on her face. Then mouthed the words, "I love you, Dad," and her face was blissful and serene. The picture faded back to a screen of static white-noise and she was gone from me.

I expected to be horrified and shocked, but I wasn't. Strangely, I felt that I understood her sense of peace and that somehow her action was part of something much larger than my own reality. I couldn't begin to comprehend the enormity of universal truth because it stretched into an infinity that my mind could not cope with. But I knew I should be happy for her. It sounds mad, but she had done what she believed to be right and I must think beyond my own selfish loss. And wasn't her ultimate aim intrinsically the same as that of Christianity? Perhaps because of this I was beginning to grasp an even deeper meaning of spirituality. After all, what if she is right? What if she really is now at peace and part of some universal spirit, helping others in some supernatural way that we mortals cannot really comprehend? Perhaps there is more than one pathway to God? Who am I to say?

It would be with me forever, that image of my Eloise smiling to the camera, saying, 'I love you, Dad.' That held me together and even helped me to strengthen my own faith in God. I believe that the essence of Christianity is spiritual love, and accepting God's love is too distant and abstract. However, love through people, who are God's creation, makes complete and utter sense to me. Because of my daughter I have truly loved and been loved, and this has helped me to love God and others more; even making me realise that maybe I never wholly did before. Love is experienced through people and she taught me more about love than any scriptural passage. Somehow, mysteriously, I have been blessed. I always thought love could never be represented by a number. But love is a number for me. Love is 351073.

And the hurricane takes me there. I enter the winds and allow them to carry me. As I rush onwards, I feel, know and understand its essence. I become it and it becomes me. Then separation, as always, causes melancholy – reminding me of my eternal solitude. Perhaps this is where I belong. The wind and the rocks and the stream are elements I understand. There is neither fickleness nor anger in their actions: unlike the selfish creatures that lurk and prowl here. I have known them; entered them; been them; tasted their instincts. All except one.

Passing through a tree I can feel its demented slowness – the aching space of nothingness. Here I can know what it is to be a home to insects, birds, mammals; what it is to be food or torn apart; even what it is to die and be reborn. But trees also know the slow bliss of beauty when they blossom and bear fruit. They sing their silent song of joy for the fulfilment of sharing their bounty for the needs of nature. Trees understand their own purpose, waiting in peace and contentment.

Water, however, is mischievous and knows its own importance. It seeps and trickles wherever it dares; its only danger is the heat and dust – the gaping maw of drought. Water seeks to be constantly reincarnated and can take on a million guises, from the warrior waves of the ocean to the dying wisps of vapour that yearn to be united and once more fall and splash in the merriment of togetherness. There are dark, tormented waters in the abyss as well as light sprinkling cascades that gently seduce the sleeping rocks.

I have dissolved into a million forms – become them all. Their instincts and their place in nature is my curiosity. Only now I am drawn onwards by a different consciousness, and my friends, the winds, have taken me to them.

My curiosity has brought me to these beings: creatures who believe they are intelligent and dominate this world. My first view is of a heaving swarm of them. But what strikes me is the chaos of their movements. Here, there is no unity like the birds that flock and fly together, always as one, in clouds that twist and tumble into ever new-forming shapes. Nor like the ants who have different working roles that create a whole. These creatures ignore each other, push and shove impatiently, unnecessarily angry – striving to beat each other. I can feel their rising irritation and worse – their insufferable and inexplicable guilt. I find myself suffocated by their aggression and pettiness. They wear multicoloured forms and seem to clutter their world with material possessions. As I look about me at the landscape I am lost in a confusing valley of mysterious square hills that surround me and seem to block out all sunlight. One of them makes a hole appear in a wall – enters in, but then contrives to make the hole to vanish again. I choose this one as my subject and follow it.

I look at the wall. This rock that I melt into is not formed as nature intended and I have to split into a hundred parts to become each rectangular stone. The elements in each small block are dying and can only just sustain my presence. I feel the torment of atrophy: certain loss of spirit from unnatural intervention, as opposed to the playful, slower changes of erosion that rock enjoys. This entry is painful and tiring, and the way through is arduous as I realise that I cannot stay here. My eventual emergence and reunion is satisfying as I knock into and brush over alien materials through which I cannot pass. Eventually I discover a long thin layer of wood, with which I merge and am accepted, there to find my temporary resting place.

One of these new beings walks right over where I lie and I feel the tension of its self-importance tug against an unrelenting fear of insignificance. Then I wonder if this dark and gloomy cave is its home. The walls and shapes are so angular and symmetrical as I begin to understand the being's need for order and regularity. I quickly pick up habits and rituals as I wait and watch. Through my observation I witness sorrow, hatred, death as these creatures are unwittingly recycled. It startles me how laughably ephemeral these creatures' lives are. Whilst I observe generations come and go, some happiness lightens the air, but more insistently there remains a bitterness that scatters over me and all around like a fine dust that gradually thickens until I feel its constricting strangle. I have to fight to overcome the growing blackness that slowly develops into a coagulated skin about me. It takes all my strength to break beyond it. Wherever these creatures walk they leave behind them a discarded skin of pessimism, and their world, unbeknownst to them, is covered as if with a layer of ash of which they remain ignorantly unaware.

Such strange objects and surfaces in this abode make moving complicated and painful. I find one subject moving rapidly in some business that evades my understanding and as I attempt to pour myself through the wooden object to which it has momentarily connected itself I find that only one small part of me can be contained within it. I try to enter into the very nature of the being but that limb of me feels tender and for the first time I understand the harshness of real pain. I retract the whole of me and keep a minute distance from my subject, having to shift when it suddenly moves towards me. I tremulously attempt the conjunction once more but a searing wound shoots through me; an excruciating bruise that throbs and stays alive for longer than I have ever known. An anguish fills me and it is fear: the feelings of this being have been transferred to me. There is a connection though, however painful, and deep within myself I feel a strange, new agitation.

There is a time when darkness descends that these creatures lay in sombre repose. Going to them as they remain still, I feel less repulsion now as I wrap myself around one of them and stealthily infiltrate its body and mind. This time, strangely, I am drawn inwards. I am both inside it and without. I can feel it and explore. In its stillness it can't feel me and I know it remains unaware of my presence. For me there is a knowingness, which penetrates me. In this act of unity a sudden rush of new strangeness fills me as I experience the thoughts and urges. Each contraction, impulse, spasm or feeling reels within me. I am suffocated by a besieging and relentless sense of distress. Then suddenly I feel myself rejected – thrust outwards as I am vomited backwards into a void. The being moves and has woken to its familiar consciousness, and from which I have been violently repelled. Once again I experience that fear – this time mixed with self-loathing. These emotions leave me pessimistic and hopeless. It is only then that I realise that this is the creature's normal state.

To allay this rejection is my goal. But it is difficult to accept or understand. I will learn to endure the straining discomfort of suffering. Our failure to sustain a connection has left me feeling strangely empty. Whilst asleep its mind is wonderful and free – when awake it is filled with an awful pettiness and such futile clutter.

Through time and tenacity I evolve, and with tireless patience I learn to abide the suffering and persist. A new fortitude engulfs me as I learn to deliquesce intolerably slowly into my subject, so that each atom of myself is plunged in agony until it reconciles and overcomes the pain, until every part of me is fully dissolved and each sensation can be borne and fully sustained. But still the suffering remains. Nothing can mask its crushing cynicism and a vague continual dread that devours any short-lived joy. It seems I cannot remain within for long.

Then I witness a ceremony in which I share and participate. My host and another creature begin to touch and stroke with great intimacy that warms me with a glow of excitement, during which their sense of ambiguous guilt still burns. Together we feel a sense of abandon as we drift into throes of sensuality. The teasing anticipation of delight becomes a gratifying thrill as I am consumed by a new pleasure more satisfying than anything I have experienced before. The two creatures rut and copulate, as I devour the ecstasy of the moment, leaving the two sweating bodies with an immediate emotion of disappointment and regret. I recognise their frustration and discontent, but am overwhelmed by this unknown sensation, knowing I have stolen the joy that was rightfully theirs.

This creature possesses the secret of such a revelation into the very heart and spirit of nature itself, but is completely unaware of it. I had been drawn in during its repose, and then again when it suffered the joys of sensual contact. There had been a moment when we connected. It was when it was distracted from its own wakefulness – when the subject realised it was more than just a corporeal entity. Many of them have no awareness of their own power and I realise that moments of oneness are quickly forgotten or rejected, just as I had been rejected.

As I continue to explore this fascinating being, attempting to make it my permanent host, I continue to be appalled by its obsession with pettiness and its overwhelming guilt – as if its only real fear is of itself or its own kind. It is then that I wonder why I am so intrigued by such insignificant creatures. Even though they continue to reject me, I still feel an affinity for it – a curiosity still draws me to it – and I refuse to be rejected. Perhaps I have already become a part of them?

"We haven't talked about masturbation yet."

Those were Toby's exact words on that first night. In bed I'd been weeping silently, pining for the loving intimacy of my parents when I heard a scuffle before being blinded by the lights suddenly glaring. I flinched as he jumped on to the end of my bed. Hiding my face from him I waved an arm in his direction, wiped my eyes and sat up. To my utter horror he sat naked on my duvet, knees pulled up to his chest. I panicked and held out both hands as if pushing away some advancing ghoul.

"Look, I'm sorry if I've given you the wrong idea, but I don't fancy you or anything … I'm not … like that …"

"Oh, piss off," he interrupted. "Even if I was gay I wouldn't fancy a posh twat like you anyway."

This made both of us giggle and relax slightly. Feeling a new camaraderie, I looked quickly at him, trying not to catch sight of his flaccid penis. He always looked unhealthily skinny and pale with bad acne on his chin, neck and shoulders. I really wished he'd put some clothes on.

"Have you ever had sex?" He asked as if offering me a cup of tea.

I shook my head expecting him to smirk but his expression gave nothing away. Instead he sniffed and considered his next words.

"My first shag was with a teacher. And she was married … to the Headmaster." We both fell about laughing.

"As you're still a virgin," Toby continued on his keynote, "you must be like me – a complete wanker. Tell me about your best one."

I won't bore you with the details, but this was his main theme on the very first night of our acquaintance. What would you have done?

Arriving at university full of enthusiasm, I found myself sharing a room with this tall, thin lad with long tied-back hair and a Celtic tattoo circling his left arm. Toby immediately welcomed me as I said a tearful farewell to my parents. Then I unpacked as he talked non-stop about his favourite rock bands and his top ten scariest movies. I'd never heard of any of them.

Our spacious room lay on the lofty top floor of a Victorian listed building. The wood panelled walls and windows leaded in a diamond lattice gave the whole place a formal dignity. Although an elegant chamber, its attractive qualities did little to make me feel better about leaving home.

As it turned out, Toby became a great roommate. He gave me my first joint, took me to my first nightclub, played stupid pranks on the other students on our corridor, thus alienating us both from the general social circle. But this made our lives excitingly secretive. So we became an arcane sect – with a membership of two.

Toby often woke me up at one in the morning, usually – and thankfully – fully dressed, and we'd go drinking or smoking in the park. This vast common was dotted with oaks and birches good for climbing, and a lake that we dared each other to swim in – even in the autumn chill. With his video camera we made execrable movies of ourselves surfing down stone steps on an ironing board, or jumping out of bedroom windows onto mattresses. We devised our own free-running route across roofs and garages that must have woken people up at night. As freshers we did little academic study – but we had a good laugh.

He even got a stunning third year Drama student to strip off completely naked in our room, by convincing her he was an artist; and got some photographs for his 'preliminary sketches'. We certainly put those to good use. When her boyfriend gave him a good beating and broke his nose, he still smiled and told me it was worth the searing agony.

At first I ignored the light flickering on and off, but it eventually got to me.

"Go to bed, you knob-end," I groaned, pulling my head under the duvet. But I could hear him whisper something and knew he'd keep going until I took the bait. I emerged from the bedclothes with eyes screwed up like an albino mole.

"What the hell is it now?" I croaked in exasperation.

The light went off and then within a few seconds came on again.

"Shit!"

I saw him standing by the light switch. Then it went pitch black. Before I could ask him what the hell he was doing, he'd flicked it back on again, turning his head like some demented lizard. He swore loudly again and switched the light off. Then it went quiet and I waited for him to move. He didn't.

"Tobes? You alright?" Just like him to feign death – waiting for gullible old me to go to him, whereupon he'd make a sudden move and thus make me jump. It worked every time. Clambering out of bed, I stumbled to the doorway and poked his soft body with my toes before finding the light-switch. I prepared myself for being scared, but when the light came on I found Toby cowering in the corner head in hands, wincing as if blinded.

"You okay? Seriously – you hurt?"

Hearing him whimper I looked down and for the first time saw a feeble, pathetic wretch. Naked and ungainly, he shivered like some lost little seal about to be clubbed to death. I helped him on to the bed where we sat together.

"Were you sleepwalking?"

He shook his head as he stared at me with those enigmatic eyes, which joined his mouth in a face-cracking smile that quickly exploded into his usual loud guffaw.

"You've been taking something without telling me, haven't you?" I looked around for any evidence of a roll-up, but saw nothing obvious; anyway I always looked after our stash, so unless he kept his own sneaky supply he couldn't be stoned either. Perhaps he'd tried something harder, although he always adamantly claimed alcohol and cannabis as his preferred toxins. (We tried magic-mushies once and vomited violently for two days afterwards).

"This is much better," he replied unhelpfully.

"What is?"

No answer.

Getting impatient with him seemed pointless as he'd explain himself in his own time and if you tried to rush him it made him even more infuriatingly vague.

"You know that pulsating thrill you get when you dream that you're falling – you jolt and wake up out of breath, your heart pumping away? It's like that – but you're awake."

"So a bit like doing a bungee-jump, then?" I scoffed.

"No, because you're safely strapped in with them." He frustratingly stopped his explanation there.

"Like watching a horror flick?"

"Bollocks, that's just someone else's idea of being scared. Only you know what really scares you, which is why nightmares make you sweat and scream out loud. The problem is you forget them. I always wanted to be able to control my dreams."

"Yeah, I've got one about some twin sisters that I desperately want to finish off."

"Not those dreams, you dickhead. I always wanted my nightmares to be real."

"Bloody weirdo!"

"Why?" he respond defensively.

"Because nightmares are usually things that you don't want to happen."

"Exactly."

"What?"

"If you can face you fears head on – confront them and deal with them – then life holds no dread for you."

"But surely fear is a defence mechanism to stop us from getting hurt or dying."

"A utilitarian argument, giving fear a function. It's more, well, metaphysical than that."

"You've lost me."

"What's man's biggest fear?"

"Premature ejaculation on a first date?"

"Arse-hole. Seriously. What are people most scared of?"

"For God's sake, I don't know."

"Yeah you do." He punched me more than playfully.

I sighed and pulled a stupid face at him. "Oh, bollocks to this ... I dunno, I give up."

"Yeah, that's just your problem isn't it?" He tapped me on the head. "Come on. Think! Think!"

"Well, I'm pretty scared of you sometimes, you psycho." He gave me a stern look. "Okay, okay – stop hitting me. Death. That's what we're all scared of. Dying."

"Oh, you do have a brain, then, you numpty? Religions have overcome fear of death in the simplest way possible." He paused to grab the bottle of Southern Comfort, took a swig and passed it to me. "Faith. Easy. Believe in the afterlife and death has no dominion. It's all up here." He tapped his own temple and bit his lips. I'd lost the thread of his discourse and I still didn't know what had shaken him up.

It remained another two days before he told me.

"It's a way of seeing those things that most frighten you."

"What?" I contained my exasperation.

Toby sighed like a schoolteacher losing his patience.

"When you confront the void."

"That's how I feel talking to you sometimes, dog-breath. What the hell you on about?"

"I've found a way of seeing things – things we shouldn't see; like a waking nightmare. I don't understand it really, but maybe what I see is from my unconscious."

"You mean your imagination?"

"Isn't that the same thing?" he asked with raised eyebrow.

"Possibly. But your imagination can just make up anything. None of it's true."

"I don't believe you sometimes." He bounced angrily on the end of my bed as I shifted my pillow to make myself more comfortable. "The imagination and fantasy are just as real as reality. We're not just physical beings that eat and work. We're minds – souls – we have an unconscious life just as thriving as our material one. Are dreams, desires and creativity just an aberration? A fault in our design?" His stare indicated this was not a rhetorical question.

"No," I mumbled.

"Too bloody right. In fact, our spiritual life is probably more important than our physical one. There's a metaphysical realm we need to explore and only by doing so will we be truly alive." After a dramatic pause he added, "I think I've seen it."

"The afterlife…?"

"Death."

This morbid fixation began to make me feel concerned for his sanity; Toby would jump off a cliff or take an overdose just to tick off the experience.

"Is that what you're doing with the flashing lights?" Ever since Christmas he'd refused to come out to the pub or be sociable, preferring to be left in the room, alone. Whenever I returned I saw lights flicking on and off. Or he'd be sat in a dark room pointing a torch in his eyes.

"Have a go. It takes a while to properly identify the fleeting glimpses." So finally, Toby meant to initiate me into his esoteric mysteries. "When you turn the light on there's a fraction of a second when you see things from your unconscious mind."

"What things?" the idea intrigued me.

"Whatever you find most horrific."

"Like monsters of the id?"

"Maybe." Toby's eyes held mine in deadly earnest.

"How do you know they're not ghosts or demons?"

He nodded whilst he considered this theory. After a long silence he finally announced his conclusion.

"What's the difference? Supernatural? Psychological? They're both real."

So he made me stand in the middle of the room and stare at a blank patch of the wall as he flicked the lights on and off. He'd fixed thick blankets over the windows to perfect the blackout and the first time

I stared into absolute darkness I felt a frisson of irrational fear. The first few times the light came on and quickly off again I thought I might have been aware of something imperceptible. It's impossible to say. Then Toby used the torch. It blinded me momentarily, but when he switched it off and then on again a tangible figure moved in the corner of my eye. I could only explain it in terms like 'lurking' or 'prowling'. I sensed it as much as saw it, leaving me with an intimidating anticipation of dread that envelops you sometimes and you just can't explain. It controls your mood, your body temperature. It sits in your stomach and affects your heartbeat. Goose pimples cling to your cold flesh and your mind can only grab at guilty or humiliating memories. The sensation of having lost all my optimism overwhelmed me throughout that same day and night.

"What did you see?" Toby asked excitedly.

"I don't know." I realised what a constant disappointment to him I must be, but had learnt not to let his stares unnerve me. "Anyway, what have you seen?"

"I've still got to identify it exactly. It takes a while to train your senses before you can begin to put things into proper perspective. I can almost touch it now. Whatever it is, it's infiltrated my mind and become like a … a kind of memory, which I now need to try and unlock."

"You mean it's something you've repressed?"

I read Toby's shrug as an admission of ignorance – something very rare.

Finally I grew bored with him. I began to make other friends and even reached a flirty-tactile stage with a girl called Sarah, from one of my seminar groups. Toby never came out. All he wanted to do was sit in a dark room and shine lights into his eyes. I spent the next few nights in Sarah's room trying to convince her to have sex with me until she relented out of exasperation.

Needing to get some clean clothes and belongings one morning, I returned to our room and found Toby cringing behind a T-bar of stage lights he'd rigged up. They looked like old floodlights borrowed from the Drama department with white numbers stencilled on them. Never had he been so pale and ill. His eyes appeared red and clogged with rheum – his skin raw with acne. Naked and smelly, he looked like a torture victim suffering from severe sleep deprivation.

The crazy fool continued gibbering and I didn't know whether to call an ambulance or run. When I spoke to him he dribbled but sounded surprisingly lucid.

"So, the prodigal son returns?" His tone was victorious. "I'm so close now. I can smell it." Toby stretched out like a languid cat, curling his toes and hunching his shoulders. "A few more trips and I'll be the man who conquered fear." I remained silent, for like any stroppy teenager he immediately did the opposite of anything suggested. As I picked up some of my belongings I became aware of him watching me.

"You're not going are you?"

"I have a date, Toby. I can't let Sarah down."

"But I've got it all set up and ready for you."

"Not now. Perhaps I'll come back tomorrow."

"No you won't," Toby sneered with curt, clipped words.

I looked at my roommate, overwhelmed with a mixture of feelings. At first shocked by his bitter tone, it only made me more determined to leave, but that was quickly diluted by a real sense of pity. Here stood my best mate: the one who first showed me how to be alive. I thought of Sarah waiting and considered all the diplomacy, flattery and wariness required just to keep her vaguely happy. The relationship with her was already fragile and unpredictable; every minute filled with pointless chatter having constantly to prove how I loved her and wanted only to be with her. She'd already expressed her jealousy about my friendship with Toby, forcing me to explain all the rumours.

On the other hand my friendship with Toby remained unconditional and exciting. I could either spend the evening talking about nothing between awkward silences, or I could venture into the unknown and discover the truth behind my ominous shadow. The thrill of the memory made me realise how things with Sarah were just wrong. I wanted to dump her, but it seemed callous after all my efforts to convince her to sleep with me. Perhaps I shouldn't have given into my lust so heartlessly.

But I did give in to my guilt. Knowing I must tell Sarah the truth, I turned away from Toby and left him to his bank of lights. As I walked off I could see them flickering under the doorway and imagined him craven and trembling in the corner, exhausted but triumphant in his perverted experimentation.

I did the decent thing with Sarah. I bought flowers and food and took her to the local park, even in overcast conditions. She giggled with excitement and called me romantic, but I didn't respond to her offers of affection, which confused her thoroughly. By the time we spread out the makeshift picnic, she sensed something was wrong, but still put her hand on my crotch; hoping physical affection might bring me round. Even though she'd dressed in a provocative outfit, I pushed her away and in a doleful voice explained my indifference.

Of course she hit me. And I deserved it. She cried, but I couldn't. Instead I stood there like a moron as she pleaded with me to reconsider things. I felt alienated from her as she told me, how as her first real love, she'd never forget me: how we'd shared something beautiful and spiritual. I stared blankly away from her and hated myself. When I offered to take her home she stormed off alone, leaving me empty.

Over by the lake I sat in the cold as the grey light slowly dwindled into dusk. Finally, the chill became too much for me. As I walked back through an avenue of pines I kept seeing movements each side of me as the surrounding darkness became more intense, but they were probably just branches moving in the wind. Perhaps bats or moths were just flittering about. It made me think of Toby and all he'd told me about fears and I suddenly felt inexplicably scared. I sprinted across the rough grass; running so fast I lost control of my feet. Stumbling over bumps and surging into ditches, I kept going at full pelt, arms ahead of me. I actually enjoyed the dread as I panicked. I guess it must be the adrenalin rush or something, but the exhilaration was fantastic. The more I ran the more frightened I felt. My imagination conjured up beasts and lunatics lunging and clawing as I dodged them. Without falling, I made it to the break in the hedgerow leading to an alley and finally the road back to civilisation. I made a strolling couple jump as I dashed unexpectedly from the alleyway and continued back towards campus.

Invigorated by this fresh experience I felt positively alive. With Sarah now in the past I became filled with a new desire. Something awakened within me anticipating Toby's experiment as if I'd just passed an initiation test. I felt the thrill of fear and wanted to reach out and touch it – to understand the joy of being scared.

As I approached the door I felt disappointed to see no lights. Perhaps Toby had finally drifted off to sleep. In the room the main lights wouldn't come on. I found my bedside lamp quickly in the darkness, but that didn't work either. I tripped over a floodlight stand, with no idea how they worked. Calling out his name, I hoped to rouse him and get some light into the stifling dinginess.

Now concern struck me. Without thinking I ripped down the blankets from the windows, letting in the light from the powerful campus security lamps. Then I allowed my eyes to refocus. At first I caught that lurking, ominous movement in the corner of my eye, but then my sight demisted as I recognised a certain shape on the floor. Toby lay prone and angular at the foot of his bed.

I fell to my knees and shook him by the shoulders, aware of something wet splashing my hands. Sweat? But this felt thick and tacky. Calling for help, I dragged him quickly out into the landing.

In the corridor the full force of the effect of seeing Toby in this state hit me. He lay naked with regular, straight, deep gashes cut into his face, torso, arms and legs, as if caught in a net of blood. His skin looked like the template for some mathematical maniac's blueprint of a crazy geometric design. The lines were perfectly executed, particularly on his face, like a tattoo, reminding me of Maori war paint. Who the fuck had done this to him?

But then I noticed his hand closed in a tight fist from whose aperture fresh blood still spilt. Wrenching it open I was shocked to find an old-fashioned razor blade sticking in to the soft fleshy part of the palm, having exposed the bones of his fingers. I carefully removed it and hurled it away, sobbing as I lifted his shoulders and hugged him. What the hell did he see?

Only vaguely aware of movements around me, someone helped me up gently and I found myself inside an ambulance watching paramedics administer a drip to an unconscious Toby.

Things worsened. Sarah reluctantly paid my taxi fare home from the hospital, as I had no one else to ask, and then told me clearly she couldn't be my friend – even though I desperately needed one. But I deserved her animosity.

Some blamed me for Toby's state; many just dismissed us both as weirdoes deserving our comeuppance. Most didn't care. So I was left alone in a room reminding me of Toby and his eccentric obsession.

Of course, curiosity got the better of me. No doubt Toby had seen or felt something which affected him greatly. That very danger remained part of its attraction. I possessed no answers, but Toby must have witnessed something that left him deranged and led to his peculiar self-immolation. Can anyone say they would not be mildly curious?

I visited Toby a number of times at hospital and was asked uncountable questions by police, counsellors and the college Governors at a special internal inquest. Toby was alive, but no longer deemed of sound mind. Psychiatrists agreed he possibly did not mean to attempt suicide, but as a possible danger to himself was kept in compulsorily by the authorities due to some Mental Health Act. The hospital's consultant psychiatrist explained how Toby suffered from endogenous depression and he also used the words 'disturbed' and 'bi-polar'. Having no immediate family he seemed shoddily treated when thrown into a modern Bedlam – a squeaky clean institution pretending to be homely – then sectioned off to solitary confinement, only allowed light under certain, controlled conditions.

I never spoke properly to Toby ever again. He died a few years later with an asinine grin fixed on his face.

After that, I attempted to build up a new life, making friends and affecting a more orthodox lifestyle; but I found the effort to socialise too onerous. With no particular ambitions my life drifted as I went through a number of failed relationships including one with a bisexual man as confused about his feelings as me. By the time I reached thirty-five I prepared myself for bachelorhood and resigned myself to middle management in a marketing agency.

This humdrum existence became a relentless routine and eventually I found myself lured back to Toby's legacy, because I finally realised what he'd been trying to show me is that the imagination is so much better than reality. I set up the necessary requirements by locking myself into my flat, darkening the windows and procuring suitably powerful lighting equipment. It's true, I remained shit-scared, but I saw this as my only step forward.

I remember squatting on the carpet, holding the lamp switch in my right hand. I blacked out the lights and before my eyes could get used to the darkness, I flashed the light quickly on again, leaving me momentarily blinded. Then I stared straight ahead, concentrating on the images in my peripheral vision. That became the real skill – to not fully focus upon the images. It took a number of flashes before the figures at the edges began to move and the brain clicked on to the correct wavelength.

I repeated the process for what seemed like hours and finally sensed the now familiar prowling menace. The shadow swayed and watched. The figure seemed to judge me. I somehow knew it was connected to me – part of me – and yet something to dread. With great trepidation I continued the ritual over and over, each time advancing closer to an understanding. The shapes and colours began to slowly focus as I put together the picture gradually shimmering into existence before me. I wasn't sure if I saw it or felt it or hallucinated, but the images became perceptibly sharper.

Then I saw it. The presence lurking in the corner of my eyes – that figure – was me.

Perhaps it signalled my early death and if I watched on it'd play like a movie steering me towards some violent demise. Surely no human could bear to watch their own end. And yet it didn't feel like a gruesome death scene. When I describe the so-called images appearing in the flashing lights, it is impossible to accurately express the sensation, as what is experienced is as much to do with emotion and premonition as with the mechanics of actual sight. My shadows possessed a tragic air, but with no sense of violence or sudden ending. More correctly, the emotion being emanated could best be described as a pervading, unrelenting melancholy.

It took three days of searching, thinking, waiting and interpreting. I suffered hunger, fever, exhaustion to my wits end. I screamed, wept and laughed hysterically; lay in catatonic states and suffered total body cramp that left my entire frame aching and weak.

Finally I understood.

I saw myself old and alone: approaching death having achieved absolutely nothing of any worth in this world. I will die a failure. This is my greatest fear: to know my life has been futile – a tragic waste. Nobody would miss me. I leave nothing of note for the world to remember me by. I have affected no one. Not one single person. It's not that I crave fame or even popularity, but I would like to have been considered special by one person, perhaps mourned for and remembered fondly. The eternal vacuum of meaninglessness engulfed me in its indifferent maw, with me a speck of dust floating pointlessly through our infinite cosmos.

So I'm left with a choice: how to respond to this horrid realisation. I could allow myself to drift into ennui or I could make something of my life. A new determination is required – for Toby's memory and honour – so his life is not wasted. I imagine his mischievous smile and his madcap plans. Even though I can never be half the man he was, and my spirit might never burn so brightly, I resolved to keep something of him within my soul and live a little. I have Toby to thank for this moment of self-realisation – this enlightenment. It took this crazy fool's death to open my eyes and see the truth of my own existence. Toby really saw something in his experiments. I know I did. It all sounds so insane, but there's something in it. Something profound that can only speak to each individual soul. And I also know it doesn't matter if it's inside your mind or beyond it; whether it's real or fantasy – because in the end there really is no difference.

WITHDRAWAL

I met Rob through an Internet dating agency. At first we swapped e-mails, sitting up into the night carefully wording answers to queries and thinking up innumerable questions aimed to be personal but not too intrusive: such as 'What animal would you like to be and why?' I was pleased with my response: 'A Unicorn – because it's mysterious and rare but worth discovering'. When I asked him to describe what he looked for in a woman, he described the very opposite of me. Therefore I assumed he wouldn't be interested in a dumpy, short brunette with no domestic skills whatsoever. I should've had more faith.

We were both scared of rejection and insecure about our appearances, but the first meeting proved a great success. Brutal honesty paid off and we each seemed keen to meet again after a long discussion over a Chinese meal.

To be honest we became obsessed with each other. Being each other's first real love, we discovered a connection both physical and emotional. Neither of us had seriously considered sex before we'd met, but now it consumed us entirely and we spent each day aching to touch the other. Neither of us bothered with other friendships.

"You put the phone down first."

"No you…"

"Okay, this time…"

"Are you still there?"

"We'll do it together…"

"I can hear you breathing … I know you're still there…"

We enjoyed watching films, particularly obscure European or Japanese movies, and joined a line-dancing class one evening a week, which culminated in a performance. It was the sharing of experiences that appealed to Rob, who wasn't bothered what he did, as long as we were together.

But I quickly realised he was becoming obsessive. He gave of himself physically and wanted to be with me like an obedient puppy, but when we were together he seemed distant and soulless: empty of emotion. We never spoke of intimate things. In fact he hardly spoke at all. But he demanded my company and of course the sex as if it was the only way he could communicate with me. It was when I realised I had no life – no friends or social life whatever I began to realise that truly loving someone meant letting them go. When I finally felt courageous enough to suggest we finish, Rob broke down in a way completely unexpected and out of character. He didn't just weep, he sobbed for a number of hours, gasping through waves of emotion and clutching himself in an agony of stomach cramps. This reaction drenched me in compassion. He spoke about the mother he never knew. He told me how she died giving birth to him – like a sacrifice. He spoke of her with tones of reverence. Her messianic status was not something to question.

"I need to tell you something," he whispered as I comforted his shaking bones.

"Of course. You can tell me anything. Sometimes it's good to say things out loud."

"It's something I've been running away from for so long. I must tell you and hope that in the telling it will help to heal my pain."

"Whatever it is, we can work through it together. I promise not to abandon you." As I said it I wondered what I really meant. I couldn't leave him after this outpouring and expression of such extreme grief.

"It happened when I was nine years old," Rob began as he smeared the snot and tears across his face. "I was walking home from school with Billy after another fun day being cheeky to teachers and playing football in the playground. As we turned in to Princess Crescent, Billy pushed me into a hedge. We were giggling and calling each other names like mates do. It was whilst being silly, not watching where we were going, that I bumped into a lamppost.

"Billy laughed and called me a 'gayboy', so I shoved him one side of the lamppost and skipped round the other way, by the kerb.

"'Takes one to know one,' I called out cheerfully.

"Without a second thought I looked up to catch the eye of my best friend, ready to call him 'knob-face' or some such name, when it took me by considerable surprise that Billy was nowhere in sight. I screwed up my eyes and looked up and down the road, spinning my head, perplexed. Opening the nearest gate, I poked my head round behind the wall, expecting to see him crouching there with a huge grin on his freckly face. We were constantly hiding from each other.

"'Oi, where are you, fart-breath?'

"No sign of him. He must have found some great hiding place. I remember being jealous not to have discovered it myself.

"I circled around a few times, trying to catch any slight sign of a movement behind a hedge or tree, or a flash of blue from his school jumper giving him away. Still no sign. Any minute now, Billy was sure to leap out at me and I'd have to admit his superiority – the champion hider. After what must have been five minutes, but seemed hours, I began to feel oddly nervous.

"'You can come out now, you ugly twat … Hey! … Billy?'

"Dawdling uncertainly and not wanting to leave the spot in case Billy suddenly reappeared, I began to think through exactly what happened. Everything had been normal, until the lamppost. I tried to dredge the events from my memory after walking round it, but I couldn't recall anything out of the ordinary. There had been no scream. I inspected the lamppost carefully, hitting it and walking round it, until I felt silly.

"As I ambled closer to home I found myself laughing as I turned into our road. Of course, Billy had merely ducked into a garden and found a short-cut home; he'd be waiting for me on his doorstep where he'd wave like he always did. It was a bit naughty of him, as we'd been told to always stay together when walking home. But then again, Billy didn't always do what he was told, particularly at school. In fact, I imagined Billy was probably watching me at that moment and laughing at me. We'd meet up at school the next day and Billy would call me a 'stupid arse-crack', or whatever the latest cool name was.

"But it was immediately obvious Billy wasn't at my house either. My stepmother, Rebecca, was in the sitting room watching television.

"'Have you seen Billy?'

"'No dear,' she frowned. Rebecca never considered Billy to be a very good influence, wanting me to make other friends.

"After tea, I panicked when I heard the voice of Billy's dad at their front door. I was aware of anxious voices that gradually rose to panic and sobbing.

"'… didn't come home…'

"'… perhaps Rob saw him…?'

"'… Robbie's been home a few hours now…' I heard my stepmother say.

"'… what the hell are we supposed to do…?'

"'… oh, God, what if something's happened to our Billy…?'

"'… I'll never forgive myself…'

"There was further crying and my parents' voices changed from tense to soothing.

"Eventually, they all sat in front of me as I shook with a guilty fear. Had it been my fault after all? I remembered pushing Billy. Had that somehow hurt him? As I spoke to the adults I was only aware of their slowly blinking eyes. All four faces held no expression, except for a few sideways glances. It seemed nobody believed my story and I couldn't sleep that night, as the flashing police lights filling my bedroom became an omen signalling something was horribly, horribly wrong.

"It made me think once again about my own real Mum. I was sure if she were alive she would be comforting me right then and I tried to imagine how that might feel. I knew Mum would be a great listener. If only I could give her a hug.

"Billy was never found.

"I was reluctantly made to attend weekly counselling sessions and because of this I found myself mercilessly teased, regularly beaten and finally completely alienated at school, which I eventually left with few qualifications. I didn't understand why I was being treated like a criminal when I'd done absolutely nothing wrong. One doctor suggested I was a delusional schizophrenic but tests proved nothing and all evidence was inconclusive. The case was declared unsolved at the inquest.

"Eventually, moving away and escaping into the dull routine of an anonymous job in an insurance office came as a welcome relief.

"On the infrequent times I visited my dad, I returned to the same place in Princess Crescent to look around for clues, or in the hope something would jog my memory. The lamppost was still there and the pavement the same with a few loose slabs. I never got an answer – there was no satisfactory conclusion. I'm just left with guilt, nightmares and stupid questions. What the hell really happened on that day?"

So we stayed together, but the relationship was frail. Rob became elusive and sometimes disappeared for days on end. But he always reappeared. Our relationship receded into an exchange of notes, emails and texts. But it was one-way traffic.

"Rob, come to The Gardener's Arms tonight at 7pm. Promise to show you a good time!"

"Rob – I miss your cute arse. Get it down to the Xmas party tomorrow night. You can have the first slow dance and if you walk me home I might offer you a coffee!"

"where r u? can b alone if u prefer??"

"tell me where ur u bastard"

"ring me im pissed n gagging 4 it"

Eventually, we spoke and he told me we couldn't stay together, without explaining why. I managed to convince him to come out with me for a meal, some quality time – just us. I felt we'd made a breakthrough as we recalled those magical first months together. He seemed to respond to my flirting and we agreed to go home. His words were pretty passionate:

"I want to touch every single inch of your body. I want you so much."

So that dark, cold evening we walked home after our meal at an Italian restaurant, our gloved fingers interlocked as our arms swung together.

"What a wonderful evening," I told him with a sigh.

"Good food, good setting and great company," Rob said.

"Well, not so sure about the last one," I teased. "For you maybe."

As Rob gave me a gentle push he stuck his tongue out at me as I squealed with mock fear.

"And now I'm going to have to tickle you." He advanced towards me with that old mischievous look in his eyes.

"Oh yeah? You and whose army?" I shoved him with a much greater force, making him stumble with surprise.

"Me, myself and I," he replied, advancing back towards me like Frankenstein's monster.

"Ooh, sca-ry."

"Right, you've asked for it this time."

Rob grabbed my shoulders and shoved me backwards into a nearby hedge, making it droop over and around me as if it was an engulfing mouth. Then the hedge catapulted me forwards into his arms and we giggled inanely before kissing in the middle of the pavement.

Just as we came up for air, I became aware of a woman walking hastily towards us with a three-wheeler pushchair, muttering angrily to herself and puffing breathlessly. I remember glancing at Rob briefly and making a face as if to say, "Hey, check out the mad woman with her formula one pram". It was clear we'd have to get out of her way. So he squeezed my hand before releasing it and, without thinking, I was forced to side-step as the pram came between us. Rob nimbly hopped around on the kerb side of the lamppost and I went the other.

"What a nutter!" I held up my hand for him to clasp it once more.

And that's when it all went weird.

Rob's eyes widened in fear and darted to each side. He seemed to stare right through me and then look about in panic. At first I thought he was joking and I punched him – with no response. I grabbed his arm, shouting, but he acted like I was not there. Exactly as I imagined he'd been when Billy disappeared all those years ago. Something felt horribly wrong, but there was no way of communicating with him. In fact he was so convincing I began to fear I had actually died and was going through an out-of-body experience.

He scanned his head round and jogged a few paces in search of me. He tried stepping back round the lamppost to see if it was any different on the other side. Rob even looked up into its orange light beaming down with a sinister buzz. It was happening all over again.

To him I had disappeared off the face of the earth. Nothing I could do made any difference. I felt so useless and insignificant. He didn't hear my shouts or feel my touch.

"Charlotte?" He screamed my name over and over.

Running after the woman with the pram he shrieked at her.

"I was with someone. Did you see where she went? Did you see her? Where did she go?" She ignored him at first, clearly in her own world, so Rob grabbed hold of her in desperation.

"Please help me. Tell me what you saw. Tell me where she went … Oh God! Please. You've got to help me!"

The woman looked shocked and screeched something back, thrashing out at him, eventually threatening to call the police. A crowd of people surrounded him and some were pulling him away as if he was a rapist. They saw me and spoke to me. It was a relief to know I hadn't died – but that didn't help Rob who was still the centre of attention.

But nobody understood how desperate he had become. The same thing – again. First he lost his Mum, then his best mate – those losses were real – and now he'd convinced himself he'd lost the only woman he'd truly loved …

The next few hours, days and weeks passed for me like a hideous hallucination: terrifying and unreal. I hadn't disappeared; it was all in Rob's mind. I wasn't lost, but Rob was – mentally lost – like an overwhelmed child who can never be consoled. I visited him many times in hospitals, wards, care homes, sheltered housing, church counselling groups. It was always futile and left me with a sense of loss.

He never recognised me again and my only way to cope was to grieve in the way one copes with the death of a loved one.

It seems Rob felt he must avoid intimacy: it became his greatest fear. As soon as he got together with and felt close to someone, for some unearthly reason they were taken cruelly away from him.

Of course it occurred to me that the childhood incident with Billy was only in his fevered imagination – some neurosis from the past. But I did some research and found all the relevant newspaper articles and court reports. Digging up all that sorrow hit me much harder than I ever could have imagined.

I was really lucky though, because I met Matty who gave me the chance to be a full-time mum to my twins. This was a blessing and helped me to distance myself from the memories. The next thing I heard through a friend was that Rob gave up work. And then he managed to frustrate all acquaintances by never replying to any calls until they all gave up on him.

Five happy years passed for me. The twins grew into healthy, bright school-children and I became a taxi driver, taking them to and from dance and gymnastics clubs. I didn't mind; I knew my place. Then one Thursday evening Matty passed me the local paper which he'd folded over onto page seven. In the bottom right hand corner was a short paragraph with a lurid headline: 'Reclusive neighbour found dead'.

> *'The body of a dead man was discovered on Monday in his living room after neighbours complained to the council about his overgrown garden and the vile, pungent smell coming through the walls. Ambulance and police forensic experts were called in and had to break into the house wearing protective suits and employing specialised equipment as the street was cordoned off. One council spokesman explained how the house was full of detritus, garbage and even human waste. "Mounds of filth in the kitchen heaved with rats and cockroaches ... The stench made us retch."*
>
> *The rotting corpse was discovered crouched in the corner of the room, stiffened with rigor mortis. Forensic reports describe how both hands were held out before him as if he was scared or hiding from something. Detective Summers told us, "Perhaps he was frightened of anyone entering his inexplicably tragic world".*
>
> *The deceased has been identified as one Robert Cobb.'*

Ray was woken up early one morning by curious, but persistent, high-pitched squeals. At first he wondered if the radiator was playing up, but then realised with a frown it could only really be one thing. Still naked he leapt out of bed and dashed across the landing to the larger bedroom now converted into his workshop. Just as he thought – specimen 1/37G had hatched.

"Damn!" He could of course snap its neck with his bare hands or maybe put it in a plastic bag and let it slowly suffocate. Then he wondered if it would block the u-bend of the toilet if he attempted to flush it away, but was put off by the image of himself prodding at the struggling, splashing creature with a bog-brush.

It tweeted innocently and he swore it blinked affectionately at him. How could he destroy such a tiny thing? The little bird had mottled tawny down as fine as fur. It wobbled unsteadily next to its broken eggshell before conveniently sitting on its typed and laminated label, which read *Larus Argentatus*.

For Ray was an egg-blower. He'd had oological articles published, even though some aspects of the work remained illegal. He could easily purchase rare eggs on the Internet and continued to make many useful contacts that way. His cabinets and wall displays contained blue, yellow, brown, spotted and plain eggs; some oval, some spherical and even cone-shaped. His favourite was the ostrich egg, as large as a rugby ball, originally one and a half kilos. Next to it sat the egg of a bee hummingbird, only half a centimetre in diameter, which proved to be the fiddliest one to preserve.

This year he decided to expand his collection of eggs to include the *Charadriiformes* order of avis: that is the gulls, auks and shorebirds. This was his first seasonal find – a Herring Gull egg. He eventually found a mating pair and lured the mother away to snatch his prize. It seems he had mistakenly thought this one newly laid and being tired that evening left it for the next day to work on. Clearly his calculations were wrong by about four weeks, which explained why he now looked down upon this orphaned baby.

It chirped again and looked at him beseechingly. Ray's heart leapt with an instinctive feeling of responsibility and without thinking picked up the soft creature which willingly snuggled into his cupped left hand. Closing his fist gently he felt the little chick's heart throbbing as it nuzzled against his fingers.

Carefully descending the stairs, Ray wondered what to feed it and how. Taking a slice of brown bread, he poured a little milk on it and found a pipette cleaned of all its chemicals. At first the little gull refused to consume the blobs of mush as it had trouble digesting, so Ray popped the mulch into his mouth and chewed it vigorously. However, this still proved inedible. So Ray swallowed the food then stuck a finger down his throat and spat the regurgitation into a little dish. After a number of attempts with the pipette again, the beak opened and Ray managed to squeeze a few drops in, before delicately cleaning its minute bill. Once he completed the makeshift nest out of cotton wool and old underpants, he placed the sleeping bird in a box and put it on the radiator, making sure the temperature remained exactly right. Only when he answered the doorbell to receive a new delivery from the postman did he remember he was still stark naked.

That night Ray sat up feeling protective and scared for its health. He needed a name and as he gazed upon the trembling chick one name struck him as perfect: Gavin.

As Gavin quickly grew up he lost his brown speckled wings and by his third summer possessed all the markings of an adult: smoky grey back, black wingtips and fierce yellow eyes. Plodding around the house on his pink, rubbery feet, Gavin was allowed to stick his golden, hooked beak in any food that Ray ate or prepared. The ornithological books seemed correct when they stated that gulls are omnivorous and this talent gave Gavin an extremely useful function about the house as a domestic waste disposal unit. He also became confidently inquisitive and noisy. During the first few years the neighbours complained to the local council a number of times, but took no action and soon the sight of Ray walking to the shops with a huge gull standing on his head became accepted and almost endearing. Ray house-trained him and taught Gavin to use the cat-flap, so he could come and go as he pleased.

That first time they went outside together without a training wire tied to the gull's feet, Ray held back fearful tears expecting Gavin to soar away forever. But instead, after a stretch of the wings and a quick glide to the rooftop, Gavin returned immediately to Ray, nibbled his ear, gave a friendly, raucous bark and flew to the doorstep to be let in. In the back garden he quickly asserted his authority over the local cats and pigeons, with which he successfully fought and unsuccessfully attempted to mate. He became a common and popular visitor in some gardens, showing great enthusiasm during neighbours' barbeques where he became particularly skilled at catching food in midair. Gavin became something of a local celebrity.

He became a regular in the local paper, particularly after his famous trip to the supermarket where he ate the entire stock of Scottish salmon on the wet fish counter. The poor young girl serving there resigned after her doctor prescribed a course of trauma counselling to help her new phobia. Then he became the mascot for the local football team. When they won the F.A. Cup, the image of him sitting on the trophy wearing a tiny scarf was seen by millions on television, whereupon Gavin then decided to fly off with the lid and really show off to the camera. It was finally recovered from the Thames by a team of police frogmen. Gavin even featured on the post-match discussion on *Match of the Day* and the clip is a perennial favourite on *A Question of Sport*.

Then one day, Ray looked at his mounting bills and impoverished bank account statements and realised the time had come to get a job so he could pay the rent and keep up with Gavin's monstrously insatiable appetite.

He found an advert for a company looking for a filing clerk, which he thought most suitable as he enjoyed being organised and orderly.

On the morning of the interview, Gavin felt restless as the usual routine had been broken. He attempted to fly around the bedroom, but only managed to knock things over and crash into the wall. Once dressed and shaved, Ray donned his best suit and firmly knotted his only silk tie. It was then that Gavin flapped up onto his head and aimed a dropping down the back of his jacket.

Undeterred, Ray locked Gavin in the bathroom.

"I'm sorry old chap, but I'll be back soon." Leaving quickly, he shut the door firmly behind him as Gavin wailed in a voice sounding horribly like a child's scream. Having no time to change, Ray waited for the bus in his soiled jacket, hoping not to be too late.

In fact, the interview went well. The interviewer, Mr. Hartfield, kept raising his eyebrows and nodding as if to indicate how impressed he was, when Ray became suddenly distracted by a tapping noise at the window. Whilst Ray wondered how the hell Gavin had got out, the interviewer repeated his question in a stern voice. Ray went red and looked up confused.

"I'm sorry, but could you repeat the question again please." Unfortunately, Ray didn't hear it the third time either. As Gavin screeched and tapped on the window, Ray was aware of the interviewer looking concerned and coming round the desk towards him.

"Can I get you a glass of water?" he heard him say.

Ray nodded.

Mr. Hartfield left the room and Ray looked back at the windowsill. Gavin had gone. Breathing more lightly now, he slowly began working out how he could explain his panic-attack when he heard an almighty explosion. The room filled with glass and feathers. Shards spilled over the desk and white plumes fluttered slowly to the floor. A long scream emanated from Gavin who wheeled around the room, causing the lights to swing violently.

"Get down here, now!" ordered Ray.

Gavin laughed uproariously as his avian 'calling-cards' splatted onto papers and over the phone on Mr Hartfield's desk.

One more shout from Ray made Gavin stop and land on his master's shoulder. As he rubbed against Ray's head and cawed softly into his ear, Ray knew he could no longer be angry.

"I'm sorry, old thing. Of course you're right. Let's go home."

By the time Mr. Hartfield returned he found his office completely trashed, his window smashed, the desk covered in bird poo and the applicant gone. This last seemed particularly perplexing as he was going to offer Ray the position.

It was clear Ray wouldn't get a real job, but he soon found it wasn't necessary, especially when a young female journalist called Brooke called to ask for an exclusive on Gavin. It seemed the national press had picked up the story after his F.A. Cup exploits. Practically overnight Gavin became a national hero. Agents fought to sign him up and he became a star on daytime television. He even ran for local election as an independent candidate; which he won before being considered for mayor. Brooke worked closely with Ray and even ghost-wrote his autobiography entitled *Uptown Gull*. With Gavin's celebrity status the money poured in, which meant they could buy a new home on the coast, where he taught Gavin how to catch fish by swooping down on trawlers.

After many months of friendship Ray proposed to Brooke on the beach, whilst Gavin scavenged for offal in a nearby rubbish tip. *Hello* magazine covered their wedding, getting exclusive rights on photographs of best-man Gavin in a dickie-bow and elasticated top hat. However, the cameras were not there that night when the three of them booked into a top London hotel.

Ray quickly discarded his clothes and hungrily unbuttoned Brooke from her corseted dress. He pushed her gently on to the bed and clambered on top, kissing her neck and touching the warmth of her skin.

"I need you so much," Brooke sighed.

And they made crazy, passionate love, made even crazier by the ear-splitting squawks coming from Gavin, perched precariously upon Ray's buttocks as the couple consummated their marriage.

Soon the noise became unbearable and Brooke pushed Ray to one side, causing Gavin to fly off the short distance to the wardrobe.

"It's no good, Ray. I can't go on like this," Brooke wept as she spoke. "I don't like to say this, but you're going to have to choose." She pointed to the wardrobe. "It's him or me."

And so Ray and Gavin enjoyed the next twenty years together in secluded bliss, living off the royalties of books, television appearances, and various merchandise. Although now in reclusion on their Caribbean island, word reached them of rights being sold by their estate for a film called *Guys'n'Gulls*.

MORE SINNED AGAINST

Adam Cook remembered a line written by some farty dead poet: "I am a man more sinned against than sinning." One of his teachers had wittered on about it, something to do with fate being cruel to some sad old twat. Anyway, that was him – more sinned against than sinning – the innocent victim.

He first met Fern through his colleague Martin who had offered him his spare room. When Adam was introduced to the other housemate he had been struck by her long dark hair and large, hazel eyes. In long, stylish velvet top with frilled sleeves and black ski pants Fern exuded an air of sexy self-confidence. Of course, she was attached: women as attractive as her always are. Adam learnt she was engaged to Canadian-born Sheldon, model and extras actor. She showed Adam a catalogue with him posing in different swimwear.

It didn't take long before he became obsessed with fantasies involving himself and Fern, along with darker ones of him murdering Sheldon in gratuitously satisfying ways. But all he could do was offer her friendship and with Sheldon frequently absent they became quite close. Martin felt left out and suspected them of having a secret affair.

"Yeah, right. In my dreams," Adam would reply, whilst Martin raised his eyebrows sanctimoniously.

Initially Fern and Adam became intimate in a frustratingly non-physical way. She would let him massage her back and shoulders, but never reciprocate nor offer any other sign of affection. In the pub or over a picnic in the park he would gaze at her lips and imagine their texture and taste. When he thought he could get away with it, he admired the shape and profile of her figure through her usually tight clothes and wondered if he could even survive the blissful thrill of touching her naked skin. Fern would often allude to their friendship in ways that left him feeling silently angry and depressed.

"Are girls and boys allowed to be best friends?" she would say with a flighty giggle. "We are just friends aren't we?"

"Don't worry," he would reply with a weary expression, "I know that a sad git like me will never be in your league."

She would hit him and giggle as if he'd just paid her an immense compliment.

"You're not sad – you're the kindest person I know."

Great! thought Adam. Bet you never say that to Sheldon. Especially not after a few hours of rough, hot passion with multiple orgasms. 'Kind' just isn't sexy.

One evening Fern appeared in Adam's bedroom as she often did before going to bed. He grasped the opportunity.

"Wine?" Adam asked hopefully. "I could get a bottle and two glasses." He didn't wait for a reply.

"If I didn't know better, I'd think you were trying to seduce me."

"As if!" Adam contained a sigh. The obvious next move was to massage her, which was the only legitimate way he had of touching her. This was like torture though – being allowed to touch her to an extent, but having to show gentlemanly restraint.

Going through the usual routine, she turned her back to him and pushed her hair away from her collar. It was all Adam could do to stop himself from pressing his lips to the nape of her neck. He wanted to kiss and touch and devour her: possess her completely.

He couldn't carry on like this, day after day.

"Do you ever dream of doing something dangerous? Something you know you shouldn't?"

"What do you mean?" She rolled her shoulders under the gentle pressure of his thumbs and sighed. He wanted to hear her sigh into his ear like that as he lay naked on top of her.

"Why are things that you know are wrong always so much more exciting?"

"What are you getting at, Adam?"

"Are you happy with Sheldon?"

"S'pose so," she said still with her back to him.

"That doesn't sound too convincing."

"I don't understand what you're trying to say. Ooh, that's good – now a bit lower."

As she didn't seem to be taking the bait, he concentrated on the massage. He gently coaxed her into lying down on her front and began to press her back with the heels of his hands.

"Would you like me to do it properly? With oils – the full works?"

"Mmm, that sounds gorgeous."

Adam decided to be confident.

"Get your kit off then." She looked back with narrowed eyes, but after a second's thought shrugged and pulled her top off over her head. It stretched and pulled her hair away from her shoulders. She was wearing a white bra that revealed a shapely cleavage and firm, full bosom.

Rearranging the pillows, she lay back down on her front as Adam poured some oil between her shoulder blades, spreading it so that his fingers slipped under the strap of her bra. Then before he could talk himself out of it, he took hold of the clasps and unhooked them. This revealed the side curves of her bulging breasts and he valiantly fought the urge to brush them with his fingertips.

Trying to focus just on the massage, he sat astride her hips and pressed deep into her back with his thumbs, finding areas that were gristly, working on those, rubbing the skin to warm up and soften the muscles.

When she gave a long, low moan it thrilled him. He continued working up and down her spine until he began to get cramp in his hands.

"Right then. How about I do your front now?"

When she didn't respond, Adam wondered if he'd pushed his luck too far. But to his amazement, Fern slowly unpeeled herself from the matress and sat up, her wonderful breasts bare, without her showing any sign of self-consciousness. Aware he was gawping and hoping he wasn't dribbling, Adam did his best to look her in the eyes, but the sight was just too magnificent for his weakened will.

"I think I've drunk too much tonight," Fern said as she propped a pillow against the wall and sat back as if completely unaware of her own nakedness.

Now why did she have to say that, thought Adam? What does she mean? 'I'm drunk so don't you dare take advantage'? Or 'I'm drunk and I'm anyone's'? Would she be like this if she wasn't drunk? He should seize the moment and ravish her, whether it's the right thing or not and sod the consequences.

He took her hands and was surprised how willingly she moved towards him. First he kissed her gently on the lips, then the neck before holding her in a tight embrace. Kissing her again she allowed his right hand to cup the rounded smoothness of her bosom. As he did so he was aware of her hands tugging urgently at his shirt so he helped her by raising his arms. The tenderness of the warmth as their skin came into contact almost caused Adam to explode with lust and he became scared that he might show himself up with someone so experienced and probably used to being with sexual athletes possessing ten times his stamina.

Once they were both divested of their remaining clothes, he surrendered to her touch and she guided him through to the fulfilment of their first time together. Adam was grateful, but slightly embarrassed and it only made him paranoid that perhaps he was the worst lover she had ever been with.

To his great disappointment she didn't stay with him into the night. His hopes of waking up next to her, still in post-coital embrace were dashed when she extricated herself carefully from under his sleepy frame, rolled him over, tucked him up and kissed him on the cheek before returning to her own room. He had been too tired to argue.

On awakening, Adam spent a few minutes convincing himself that it had not just been a dream, then wondered if it would be romantic to creep into Fern's room and seduce her in her bed. All logic went against the idea. What if she woke up and regretted last night? She had said she was drunk after all. It was then that he remembered that she was engaged to that arsehole and that he had had no right in the first place to move in on somebody else's girl. It had just been a one off – a fantastic memory for him to treasure. Closing his eyes he tried to remember her nakedness and the smooth firmness of her flesh. But this lovely image kept cloying with the more realistic thought that their friendship had been ruined and that he might have to consider leaving the house.

A knock at the bedroom door allayed his growing despondency and he half expected Sheldon to appear with a baseball bat aimed at his skull. Instead, the pleasant surprise of seeing Fern, still in her skimpy pyjamas holding a tray knocked him sideways.

"Hiya, Cassanova," she smiled, pushing him aside to sit next to him.

"Wow," Adam said, rising stupidly and trying to take it all in. "A bacon sarnie?"

"Yup. And you just wait 'til I show you what I can do with a sausage…!"

Three days later Adam had been sitting in his office listening to the most boring salesman on the planet whinging on about how Adam's company were their company's 'priority customers', whilst Adam was wondering if the guy would notice if he shut his eyes for a minute, when the phone went. Usually, he wouldn't answer it with a client present, but desperate for a distraction he apologised.

"I'm expecting an important call."

On the other end he heard an American accent splutter in a harsh tone:

"D'ya love her then?"

"Excuse me?"

"She told me she's in love with you."

It took a few seconds to compute. Sheldon.

Adam looked at the client who was tapping figures into his palm-top and wondered how he could deal with this and not lose his financially advantageous custom.

"Um, how did you get my number?" he asked tentatively.

"Don't you understand?" the voiced whined pathetically. "She's mine. How could you do this to me?"

"Well, isn't that really between you and her?"

"But she's mine."

"Erm…no, actually. She can make her own decisions." Adam faltered slightly, keeping half an eye on the fidgeting salesman. "What exactly has she told you then?"

"That she's leaving me for you."

His heart leapt with a thrill but he had to choose his words carefully.

"Then perhaps you should accept her decision," he ventured. But then to his utter horror, Sheldon broke down and sobbed loudly into the phone. Adam held the receiver at arm's length for a second and made a face to the client who looked at his watch unsubtly. Adam held up his index finger to signal that he'd be with him in one minute.

With some reluctance he then put the phone back to his ear to hear Sheldon sniveling.

"…and no-one else will ever love her as much as I do. We're so right for each other. You don't know her like I do…"

"Right…um…I have to go now," Adam pulled a face for the salesman's benefit. "Perhaps we could speak later…"

"You didn't answer my question," continued the whining voice. "Tell me do you love her?"

"How I feel has got nothing to do with you." Adam felt trapped.

"I want to know that the man she's chosen will take care of her and treat her properly."

"You need have no fears about that…" Adam said with an air of finality. "I have to go now…"

"I want to hear you say it."

"Sorry?"

"I want you to tell me right now down this phone how much you love her."

"Look this is silly now. I can't do that."

"Why are you there with someone?"

"Ye-es."

"Then just answer yes or no."

Adam knew he should just have put the phone down, but he was trembling slightly and even beginning to feel sorry for Sheldon now. The poor guy was just in love with Fern – and who could blame him? Adam also did still feel bad about sleeping with someone else's fiancée.

"Be quick then. I have a client waiting."

"Do you love her? Yes or no?"

"Yes, of course."

"Are you going to marry her?"

"Look, I'm going to put the phone down now…"

"Do you know all the little things about her, though? The way she breathes when she's asleep. How her beautiful eyes glitter with joy when I read her poetry. Her determined smile when she walks through the rain…"

"Sheldon, I'm putting the phone down…"

"…her graceful hands as they…"

"Goodbye."

Adam's mind was doing a loop-the-loop, but he managed to turn to his visitor and smile.

"Right then, where do I sign?"

Adam promised Fern that he would become a better lover with more practice and then realised how pathetic that sounded. But practice they certainly did. The thrill of her urgent and constant needs had amazed him at first and he couldn't believe his incredible luck. Before he'd met her, he'd only ever had sex once, and that had been frustrating and vaguely unsuccessful. But great as the sex was with Fern, their relationship flourished and became more emotional and profound. They were each other's best friend. Her hunger for his emotional love and support was as insatiable as her lust. For two years they were happily married – but then her father died.

Even though Fern wasn't particularly close to her dad, his death had a big effect on her. The reason why Adam had never met his father-in-law was because he had been involved in some strange religious community in London called 'Not of This World' that refused all contact with 'sinners'. Fern went to the funeral alone as Adam wasn't invited.

Instead Adam found himself on a stag weekend in Dublin that basically involved two days of non-stop drinking. Martin went plus another guy he knew from squash. It was a chance to utterly switch off, enjoy a bit of fun, tell a few jokes, be irresponsibly rude and disorderly and even flirt a little. They began drinking before they even got on the plane. Mid-flight the hostesses were happy to serve them with beer and as soon as they landed they found the nearest pub to begin their forty-eight hour pub-crawl.

None of them remembered their return flight on Sunday, let alone how they even got on their plane. Adam woke up just before landing and found himself looking forward to seeing Fern. By the time they had alighted and retrieved their luggage he felt completely sober. It was easy enough to get a train and taxi home

Whilst the weekend had been a good laugh, he couldn't help feeling that it was nice to return to the happy comfort of his real life. Fern was familiar and even an essential part of him – without her he was just incomplete. The drunken madness and inane conversation had been great for a couple of days, but if he was honest Adam was looking forward to drinking a cup of tea and doing the washing up

As the front door swung open he had hoped to see Fern standing there smiling. It occurred to him that he should have bought her some flowers – but then again that might have looked like he had something to hide.

He put down his case and pushed open the living room door. She was sat on the sofa, watching television.

"Hello, my darling. I've missed you."

"Hi." Fern stayed sat down and continued watching the television screen.

"You're a sight for sore eyes." Adam tried a different tack.

"Serves you right for drinking too much."

"Sorry?" Adam asked, taken aback.

"If you've got sore eyes then it's your own fault." She still didn't look up.

"Oka-a-y," Adam ventured. "Have I missed something here?" He stood between her and the television.

"Mmm?" Fern replied, leaning to one side to peer around him.

"Are you okay?"

"Yup."

"Have I done something wrong?"

"No."

The silence grew into a fearful tension as Fern watched the end of her programme, whilst Adam went upstairs, confused, to unpack.

Fern had never been the most expressive person in the world, but her silence and cold, determined face signalled that something out of the ordinary had happened. When he put his hand on her shoulder and was met by her expressionless eyes his heart sank.

"Is it someone else?" Adam had often felt he wasn't quite enough for her. "You've met someone else haven't you?" he became more insistent.

"I'm not having an affair if that's what you mean."

This came as a relief, although it didn't explain her strange behaviour.

"But something's happened hasn't it?"

Fern just nodded and began to walk away. He caught hold of her arm.

"What the hell's going on?"

She turned to him with a pained look in her eyes. "It's not your fault."

"What's not my fault?"

"I have met someone."

"Who…?"

"God!"

His mind went blank.

"When I went home on Saturday and got baptised," she added.

"Home? But this is your home."

"To Dad's. I understand now that only through redemption can we find eternal life. Don't you see? Dad is now an angel watching over me and he has called to me to be saved. Dad spoke to me. He showed me how to get healed."

"Your dad spoke to you?"

"You see, I knew you wouldn't understand. I don't need to explain all this to you. It would just fall on deaf ears."

"Of course I'll listen to you. I'm your husband."

"Not any more."

"You what?"

"You're not one of the chosen, so our marriage is null and void. That's what Craig explained to me."

"Who the hell's Craig?" This was becoming a little too bizarre and Adam started to panic.

"Craig is one of the apostles – my mentor. He and his wife, Joy, are discipling me. He has the gift of prophecy. It was Craig who heard my Dad and helped me to listen. Craig is my Dad's best friend. They grew up together."

He realised he should not have let her go to the funeral alone. Why hadn't it occurred to him?

Adam sat down and kept his concerned eyes on his wife, but he wasn't sure that he recognised her. He had absolutely no idea what to say to her.

"I shall be leaving in four day's time."

"Leaving? Where are you going?"

"To live with Craig and Joy."

"Why?"

"I can no longer dwell with an unbeliever."

And that was the only explanation she would give. He discovered that she had already packed a small case. When Adam tried reasoning with her, saying how much he loved her, she only shook her head in pity. When he tried holding her she pushed him away as if he was trying to rape her.

"I knew you'd be like this," she said, coldly. "'Be ye not yoked together with unbelievers – for what communion hath light with darkness?'"

With the case in her hand she left the house and he fell onto their bed and wept. Adam had no idea where she had gone or if she'd be back. As most of her things were still in place he assumed she would collect the rest of her belongings at another time.

That night he sat up going through their conversation in his head and trying to work out exactly what had happened. Everything had been fine before he'd gone to Dublin…or had it? Perhaps he'd missed something – some clue – and once again misread the signs.

When she didn't return the next morning, which he'd taken off work, he decided to talk to Martin who had sometimes been known to infrequently attend a church. It was his best shot. Adam phoned him on his direct work line.

"Adam? Got a bit of a hangover have we?" Martin laughed into the phone. "Can't take your drink, eh?"

"Martin, shut up and listen. It's Fern. She's left me and I've got no one else to turn to." There was a short silence. "You know her as a well as anyone. I need to talk…ask you a few questions."

"Sure, mate," Martin's tone became serious. "Anything to help. Sorry to hear it."

"It's complicated. She's gone all religious on me. I was hoping you'd understand – you're sort of into that as well aren't you?"

"Well, I was brought up as a good Methodist and have been known to go to church at Christmas and Easter – if that's what you mean. But I'm not exactly the Pope."

"She's got involved in some church and she's not allowed to live with me because I'm an unbeliever. She seems to think that her dad spoke to her as an angel or something."

"Um, well that doesn't sound like orthodox Christian theology to my mind," Martin said ponderously. "Sounds like it might be some weird sect or cult. Strange. That really doesn't sound like Fern…"

"Exactly. There's something weird going on." Adam tried to keep his voice level. "I feel like I'm in some twilight zone."

"Okay, mate, you hang in there. I'll come over right after work. Tell me more about this church."

But Fern appeared before Martin. The sound of the front door being opened was followed by voices. Still in his dressing gown he jumped up and got to the hall to see Fern accompanied by a severe-looking lady in her fifties, smartly dressed and with tied back grey hair.

"There he is," Fern gestured to him and the lady scowled in his direction.

"Where's your stuff, then?" the lady asked with complete disinterest. "Upstairs?"

"Yes, first on the left," Fern replied, looking away from her husband.

"Will you be alright?" She nodded towards the incredulous Adam as if he were a stain on the carpet.

"Yes, thanks. I'll call if I need you."

As the lady pushed past Adam he couldn't help but make a grab at Fern.

"Who the hell's she?"

"Please don't blaspheme," ordered the lady sternly. "And let go of her this instant." Adam was unsure why he was obeying her.

"Who do you think you are coming in to my home and telling me what to do?" Adam demanded.

Fern stepped between them. "It's okay. This is Joy. I told you about her and Craig. He's the apostle who helped me to see the truth and now they are teaching me to read God's Holy Word. They're even giving up their home so they can disciple me full-time. It's a great honour."

"You'll be living with them?"

"Yes, then when I'm ready I'll be baptised and married…"

"Married? But you're married to me."

The lady – the badly-named Joy – took control again.

"I'm not leaving you alone with him. You get your things and then we'll leave this madhouse." She turned to Fern. "Remember – 'the unbelieving are as murderers and whoremongers that shall have their punishment in the lake which burneth with fire and brimstone'."

Fern nodded dutifully and dashed upstairs. It was clear that Adam wasn't going to get past this woman to talk to his own wife. Something flashed through his head. Was this the last time he was ever going to see her? It also occurred to him that being aggressive was only going to alienate her further so he tried to calm his mind and think of a better tactic. He couldn't just let her go – this was crazy.

"Please let me talk to Fern – alone. Just for a few minutes. Don't you understand? I love her."

"You cannot stand in the way of God's plan for her. She will soon be betrothed to another."

Adam felt physically sick.

"But you can't do that. She's married to me. Don't you see? If she marries then it won't be legally recognised. I won't agree to a divorce."

"We care nothing for your worldly laws and do not recognise the authority of your government. The only authority comes from God as written in the Holy Scripture and from the mouths of his prophets. God has spoken to Fern and she is obedient to his way."

Who was he to argue with God? He felt so helpless and confused that all he could do was cry, which Joy interpreted as the will of God overpowering this sinful unbeliever.

As Fern got to the top of the stairs she was met with the image of her husband sobbing loudly on his knees. At first she thought he was penitent and had heard the call of the Almighty, but then she heard his sinful voice calling her to stay.

Joy took hold of her case and pushed her towards the front door. As they passed the weeping man she muttered, "Get thee behind me Satan." Then in Fern's ear she whispered:

"Do not be as Lot's wife who looked back at Sodom and Gomorrah and was punished. Step forward in faith as both your fathers in Heaven command."

As the two women stepped over the threshold they spoke in weird voices. Adam didn't understand a word his wife was saying.

Martin seemed to be the only friend who could help him.

"I looked up the name of this church on the internet and they're bloody weird if you ask me."

"You believe in God. How do people get like this?" Adam asked without thinking.

"Oi! Excuse me," Martin chuckled as he finished his pint. "Just because I believe in God doesn't make me a weirdo. I think Protestant Christianity is extremely normal, thank you very much. People usually laugh at us because we're boring – not because we're lunatic, brainwashing fundamentalists. The church is usually criticised for being too liberal and nice. You can't have it both ways, you know. I have absolutely no idea how they managed to get Fern like that. They don't worship the same God I do – let's get that straight right now."

There was a pause as Adam peered into his empty glass.

"Sermon's over," Martin announced. "Now let's get pissed."

Adam took time off work, deteriorating in a spiral of depression. Imagining that he would never be happy again. Three months of unhappiness passed.

It was as he was watching a DVD on his own with a can of bitter and some nachos that the doorbell rang in three short bursts. Adam opened the door to a smartly suited businessman in his fifties. Usually he enjoyed being rude to salesman, but tonight he just wanted to be left alone.

"Mr. Adam Cook?" the man asked in a jovial manner, hand outstretched.

Adam sniffed. "What do you want?"

"I'm here representing Miss Fern Macey."

He jumped on hearing the name. So she had reverted to her maiden name already. Adam felt his heart sink and the old bile of panic rising to his throat.

"As your ex-spouse she is entitled to half of all your possessions, including all property and shared assets. We would like to proceed with an amicable settlement, preferably out of court. She felt sure that you would comply."

Staring with disbelief at the announcement, Adam stood in silence for a few moments carefully considering his options.

"You say 'ex-wife', but legally we're still married."

The man smiled. "Miss Macey has begun filing for divorce and you would do well not to make things difficult. She will cite physical and mental abuse as her reasons if you put up any barriers, Mr Cook."

Adam laughed. "But that's lying. Does your God condone lying? Isn't that a sin?"

"God moves in a mysterious way, his wonders to perform."

"Especially if there's a bit of cash involved, eh?"

"I had hoped that we could settle this in a friendly way, Mr Cook. For Fern's sake."

Just hearing her name filled him with pent up grief.

"Tell Fern that I'll only settle things if I can talk to her directly. I'm not going to stand here and talk to you about my private life. Who are you anyway?"

"My name is Craig Merwyck."

So this was the great apostle. Adam wanted to punch his lights out there and then. But what would it solve? It would only give these people evidence for a quick divorce settlement. He thought carefully as he spoke.

"I love Fern and would do anything for her. Tell her I'm willing to meet her on her terms to talk this through."

"I'm afraid you wouldn't be alone. You could only speak to her in the presence of a chaperone."

"I understand," Adam nodded. "Perhaps she could tell me more about this God of yours."

Craig Merwyck's eyes narrowed. After careful inspection of Adam's face he nodded and stuck out his hand as if sealing a business deal.

"I'll speak to Fern and to the other Apostles then get back in touch with you. Goodbye."

The man strode purposefully out of the gate and towards his parked BMW, which faded quietly into the distance.

Two days later he answered the phone to hear Craig's voice.

"Mr Cook? Miss Macey is happy to meet with you, but only on our terms."

"That's fine," Adam answered. He was given a date, time and house address in North London.

Using his 'London A to Z' the next day, Adam took the train, tube and then walked to the given address. The walk took a little longer than it seemed it should have on the map. Luckily he had given himself plenty of time and arrived half an hour early.

With growing confidence and determination he knocked on the door. It was a perfectly ordinary end of terrace Victorian house with bikes and children's toys littering the front garden. A number of voices could be heard talking inside as he stood waiting.

Eventually, an elderly lady opened the door.

"Mr Cook?"

Adam nodded.

"Could you come this way please." She stepped out of the door, closing it behind her and motioned for him to enter the side passage whose gate was wide open. There he saw a sign that pointed to the 'Church Office'. He let her lead the way and found himself at the back door that led into a large kitchen. A dog on a leash barked as he approached. Two ladies were washing up and he recognised Joy who looked up and muttered something unheard to her companion.

"If you would wait here, please." The older lady then disappeared through a door leaving him with the two who continued washing up in silence.

Adam looked around but saw nothing out of the ordinary.

When the lady returned he was relieved to be directed into the office where Craig Merwyck motioned for him to sit down in a big leather armchair.

"Mr Cook. Good to see you again." Craig sat down behind his desk and officiously riffled through some papers. "I trust we can come to a happy compromise."

"I did say that I wanted to speak directly to Fern."

"Yes, yes. Quite. She'll be here presently." Craig cleared his throat and leant forward. "You mentioned something about searching for God. Now perhaps you would like to pray with someone. Or perhaps read one of our tracts."

Although both sounded terribly dull to Adam he murmured an interested sound.

"Perhaps Fern could explain things to me…"

"That wouldn't be very suitable, I'm afraid."

"Why?"

"Well, Miss Macey is at an early stage in her own spiritual development and still needs guidance as she seeks to understand God's truth. We would link you with an apostle who would become your friend and prayer partner. A man of course."

"Perhaps I should just see Fern and then I can be on my way."

Craig pressed a button on his desk.

When Fern finally appeared, Adam had not been prepared for such a transformation. Her long dark hair had been cut to a boyish bob, she wore a long black skirt and an unflattering brown top with a collar that folded under her chin. Her eyes had no sparkle and her face was drawn in.

Without thinking he stepped towards her but as he did so she flinched back and immediately looked to Craig for help. When he nodded to a chair in the corner she sat down on it.

"Hello Fern. How are you?" Adam felt a horrid mixture of delight and trepidation at seeing her. He sat back down and watched Craig nod as if to allow her the right to respond.

"Hello."

Is that it? thought Adam. You were my wife, lover and soul mate and that's all you can say to me?

"I love you, Fern," he stated quickly.

"Now look, Mr Cook. We're here to talk about the money…" Craig asserted.

"No, I'm here to talk to my wife," Adam said raising his voice.

"Now let's stay calm…" Craig began. Adam ignored him.

"Fern, I love you." He knew he sounded desperate but no longer cared.

"No you don't. If you loved me then you would also love the Lord and repent of all your sins." Fern spoke in a measured tone.

"But I don't understand why you had to leave me. We could have talked about faith and God. We could've gone to church and found out together if I'd known you felt this way. Why does it have to be so extreme? Please, come home and let's talk it through in a rational way."

"I can't," Fern said simply.

"Can't? Who says? Him?" Adam pointed to Craig.

Fern smiled and looked at Adam as if he was an ignorant child.

"God told me to leave you." Fern looked at him unblinkingly.

"How do you know it was God?" Adam wanted to scream with frustration.

"I heard my father speak to me. Angels are messengers from God. 'Are not all angels ministering spirits? saith theLord.'"

"What on earth are you talking about?"

"She's quoting scripture, Mr Cook, the living word of God," Craig explained from his seat behind his desk. Adam turned to him.

"The Bible? But it was written by men…"

"All scripture is God-breathed, Mr Cook. You might not like it, but it is the only path to righteousness and eternal life. If you choose not to enter the strait gate then you must face your own damnation when you come before the Lord."

When Adam didn't respond, Craig smiled and took the advantage.

"I will pray for you, Mr Cook," Craig said, getting up, "after we have signed those papers."

"Fern," he pleaded directly to his wife, "let me talk to you alone just for a few minutes. Please. It's me – Adam. I won't hurt you. I love you."

She looked at him and then at Craig.

"It's okay," she said to Craig. "For a few moments. I'll take him to the kitchen."

He nodded his assent, but followed them out. Before leaving them Craig whispered to the two ladies who left the washing up and went out the back door. Then he took one of Fern's hands and spoke gently to her.

"I shall be right here and Joy and Daphne are in the garden if you need us. Okay?"

Fern nodded and he left. Letting her go into the kitchen first, Adam carefully closed the door and then stood in the middle of the linoed floor. From there he could see the two grey haired ladies throwing a stick to the dog now freely roaming the back lawn.

"Why have you come here, Adam?"

This was the first time she had used his name and it made him smile.

"To see you, of course."

"You shouldn't have come."

"Why not? Do you still have feelings for me?" Adam's heart leapt at this glimmer of hope.

"Are you here to test me?"

"I want to understand what you're doing. It doesn't make sense."

"'The light shineth in darkness; and the darkness comprehended it not.'"

The same irritation crept back. "What do you mean?" his voice had become whine. "What, am I some kind of evil demon to you?"

"'If thy hand offend thee, cut it off,'" came the answer neat and simple. She was now sitting on the yellow worktop, swinging one leg against the cupboard beneath it.

"Then you find me offensive?" Adam's head was in a whirl again. How hard it was to think straight when faced by such a lack of emotion; such surreal answers. "Why do you have to leave me and never see me again?" Adam pursued his point. "Can't we have a proper conversation? You never even gave me a chance to work things out or to change. You just went and left me to… to…" He gasped with a surge of infuriated confusion. His feelings were inexpressible.

"It's not hard to understand," Fern replied, looking away from him and out into the garden. "God found me through my Dad and his message was clear to me. He speaks to me, Adam. Dad speaks to me every day."

"Your dad is dead." She smiled serenely and shook her head. "How does he talk to you?"

"Through Craig."

"So you believe him? What if he's lying?"

"Craig is a prophet – a holy man of God. The spirit speaks through him. Just as there were prophets in scripture there are still prophets among us today – don't you see? God still loves us now and he wants to speak to us. Your doubt and disbelief are just further signs that you work for the enemy. You came to change me and mock me ... but 'Blessed are they which are persecuted for righteousness' sake: for theirs is the kingdom of heaven'."

"But what about 'God is love' and 'love your enemy' and all that? Is that all out the window?" Adam creased his forehead trying to remember some of the things Martin had mentioned to him.

"You have such a limited knowledge. You just choose the parts you want to believe in. Faith is not like a pick 'n' mix, Adam. It takes a lifetime of dedicated training to fully understand…"

"But shouldn't it be simple – for everybody?"

"No because only certain people are chosen." She said this with a hint of boredom in her voice. It was perfectly clear she wanted him to leave, but Adam wasn't willing to make it so easy for her.

"So if I'm not chosen then I'm damned anyway?"

"It's complicated but yes, something like that."

"Oh, thanks a lot." Getting no response he decided to change subject. "So you want to divorce me?"

"I would like to marry a true believer and begin my own family."

"Is there someone?"

Fern paused before answering. "Sheldon is back. He was baptised yesterday."

Adam was suddenly filled with a searing jealousy. She was finally lost to him.

He turned to Fern with a desperate expression

"But you're my wife. Doesn't the vow you made mean anything to you?" She continued to watch the dog in the garden.

"I know we had something once. But it's over now." She spoke with an air of finality. "I know you're a kind man – but it's not enough now. I may regret it but it's something that I have to do."

His mind replayed what she just said: 'May regret it…' Was that a chink? Did she still have some hidden feelings for him? Seeing her there with her dark hair he recalled how beautiful she was and without thinking reached out a hand and touched her breast.

He knew it was the wrong thing to do.

She looked shocked, but he needed her so badly. Just as he leant in to kiss her, Joy returned and was pulling him away and calling for reinforcements. Two men he didn't recognise came in and dragged Adam into another room, pinning him to a chair. He should've just walked away with his dignity intact, but instead he lost control.

Kicking, screaming and writhing, he cursed and shouted at them all. He used every single expletive known to man. They fought back with surprising strength, too. Adam felt himself punched in the stomach and between his legs, which made him howl in rage and agony. Eventually he was pinned on the floor in the hall by six hefty men. He couldn't see Fern any more, but Craig was hovering about directing his troops.

Even though he felt light-headed, Adam continued shouting and then to his own shame, broke down and convulsed in a tear-drenched frenzy. As he wept pleas of desperation to Fern begging her to take him back and struggling against the strong grips of the men, Adam heard them praying for him – in tongues. They sounded drunk as they sang in strange lilting tones. They adopted stern, grave looks on their faces, talking in hushed tones, as they tried to exorcise the demons from their victim. Adam cursed himself for playing into their hands. How they must have loved this. Here on their own territory they had some demon-possessed heathen whose behaviour merely confirmed all their suspicions about how sinful non-believers are.

Eventually, he was carried to a car and driven all the way home. It took an hour and a half to drive him there as he just snivelled in the back. One giant of a man escorted him limping to his own front door.

"Don't ever think about returning or we'll have you put away. We could get you for breaking and entering, rape, GBH – you name it. We have lots of witnesses and you have no alibi. Fern hates you and never wants to see you again. You'll be hearing from our lawyers." The man watched him open the door and continued in his quiet menacing tone. "She'll be moving house soon, too, so don't bother trying to find her." The man moved off down the path.

"She's married to God now," he called over his shoulder as he got back into the car and drove off.

The papers came through for a quick divorce and Adam – a broken man – signed them. He took out a second mortgage to pay the settlement. It felt like a bereavement: and he had to confront the loss.

More sinned against than sinning – that was him – the ultimate victim. What had he ever done to deserve all this?

His worst enemy was his own imagination. The image of her married to Sheldon haunted him everywhere. At work he couldn't concentrate as he kept thinking of him touching her and slobbering over her – Fern – his own dear Fern. This became a constant torment he couldn't dispel, as if some vengeful spirit, obsessed with torturing his innocent soul, now possessed him.

On their website he read of their missions to plant new churches in Manchester and Newcastle, and wondered if he should travel north to find her. But what could he ever hope to achieve? It would only end in his frustration and a confirmation to her that she did well to leave such a loser.

And so many months passed in self-pity in his attempt to build up a life again from nothing. Self-help books provided ephemeral sound bites with great meaning late at night, but seemed empty and pointless the next morning. Whisky became his best friend and only companion for a number of weeks until his doctor told him to change his diet and life-style. Helpful colleagues matched him up with single friends to no avail as he couldn't bear to hear their tortuous stories, which only reminded him of what he was attempting to forget.

When it seemed that he couldn't get over his sorrow, he was called in to see the Personnel Manager and MD who offered him an attractive redundancy package giving him a number of months of financial-free worry whilst he looked for another position. They also offered to write him a positive reference. It was meant well and he had no choice but to accept it.

Then one cold day the phone rang as he ate his lunch.

"Hello? Adam?"

"Fern?"

A confusion of emotions churned up inside him.

"Adam, I want to come home. I realise this is a long shot and I'm probably the last person you want to see. You probably hate me but I need to see you. I need your help – I don't have anyone else to turn to."

So she needed him now did she? Just as he was getting his life in order and sorting out his feelings she was going to come back and rip his heart in two, all over again. His sense of foreboding was immense and he needed to think clearly.

"Where are you Fern?"

"I'm at the airport. I'll get a taxi…"

"No wait," he said quickly. "I'll come and get you. Be at Arrivals – you know, where you get the taxis."

"Oh. Okay. If you're sure then."

"Just be there."

Something wrenched and tugged away at his innards as he drove there. Would she be alone or with Sheldon? He didn't know what he'd do if he was there too.

As he drove up the ramp to Arrivals he peered amongst the groups of people. Then he saw her. She stepped off the kerb between two taxis and raised an arm. He stopped suddenly, causing the car behind to swerve and beep angrily. Fern opened the passenger door and climbed in. He hardly had a chance to look at her before pulling off. Having to concentrate on driving, he had absolutely no idea what to say to her. Obviously, Fern felt a similar awkwardness and apart from thanking him remained silent as she shifted uncomfortably, pulling her skirt over her knees and nervously picking bits of fluff off her lap.

Once home, he parked the car in his usual space and applied the handbrake, Adam sighed and turned to his ex-wife. He could hardly believe she was right here next to him. This moment had been one he had imagined over and over – had practised a million times – and yet now he was feeling dizzy.

"Come on in."

In the living room, she perched herself on the edge of the sofa whilst he made her a cup of tea.

"How was the flight?" He wanted to get the formalities out of the way first.

"Awful," she replied. "I was sick the whole way."

"You're looking good, Fern," he said tenderly, putting the tea on the table beside her.

"Liar." She managed a smile.

She had put on a lot of weight and looked pale.

"I shouldn't have flown, but I had to get away."

"Tell me what happened," Adam said sitting next to her and putting his arm round her. She shivered put didn't shrug him off. In fact she pressed in a little closer. "You can tell me anything, you know that don't you?"

"I just need to know one thing."

"Okay."

"Do you still love me?"

"Blimey, that's quite a question!" He paused and looked down at the ground. "I love you more than anything in the world."

"Then I need your forgiveness."

Adam nodded and fought back the tears that now blurred his vision of her.

"I'm pregnant, Adam. I'm pregnant…and I'm so sorry." With that she collapsed in a long convulsion of tears and he held her as tightly as he could as if he would never again let her go.

"What about Sheldon?" he asked when they had wiped their faces and as she was sipping her tea.

"Sheldon? Oh, I've no idea. I never saw him again after he was baptised. I don't know where he went. I went to Toronto with Craig and Joy. This baby is his."

Adam understood hate for the first time in his life. He could picture the man now and he just knew that that face would never be erased from his memory.

"Craig's baby," Adam said more as a statement than a question. He should have guessed. "Does Joy know?"

"Yes. Craig chose me as his handmaiden. Joy couldn't have children."

"So she let her husband have sex with you?"

"It's God's way as written in the scripture."

"You don't still believe all this do you?" Adam felt the resentment rise again.

"I'm so confused now. I don't know what I believe."

Adam's mind was filled with the horrific image of Craig with Fern.

"And because he told you God said it, you went along with it?"

"At first I thought I had no choice. I believed I'd been chosen… oh…it's so hard to explain and it sounds so stupid now." She paused. "You see, he was Dad's best friend. My only link to him. I miss him so much." She sat back and closed her eyes. "I understand if you hate me and I'll go if you want me to."

"No, no, it's all right, Fern. I don't hate you." It was Craig he hated. The phrase "more sinned against" came into his head again. "I just want to try and understand why you did these things." Adam also closed his eyes and felt helpless.

"I didn't want to."

The meaning of what she just said struck him hard.

He wondered if there were enough tears in the world to express their sadness. "I'll kill him. We should report him. That bastard should be in prison."

"No, no. There must be no hate. I just want it all to stop. I want things to be like they were."

Adam wasn't sure that would ever happen. No, it would never be the same. Many sins had been committed, but whose sins would be forgiven? Who was more sinned against?

"I love you, Fern. We'll work it out together – as long as it takes."

And he held her carefully in his arms, uncertain about the future.

DELIRIUM TREMENS

Donny felt himself lifted and carried like a rolled up carpet.

"Get off! Leave me alone!"

Kicking and struggling, his foot connected with something soft but he was swiftly and very painfully overpowered. His head ached as the world outside burst into flames. A cold hand gripped his stomach and wrenched him inside out. This was the craving – the desperate need. He had to hang in; ride the torment; burst through and face the demons. Then he tumbled into the burning abyss.

Donny's body lay inert, drained of strength and energy – poisoned. When he tried to talk he couldn't, because they had cut out his tongue. Was he now trapped in some inner sanctum; on an altar table to be sacrificed? He could not shout out in pain as they slowly sliced his flesh and left him to bleed. What delicious and cruel torture. To inflict hideous acts of sadism but allow no expression of agony. To die silent and dumb. To fade in mental torment, unheard – driven to distraction by the inability to voice those deepest fears. His heart burst with the terrifying brilliance of their methods – denying him the basic right of being in pain. He tried to rouse himself, but he felt weaker and weaker …

But this couldn't be death. Donny grew aware he still possessed a solid body. He now lay in a black room, wet sheets tangled round his feet. His neck felt stiff and sharp pincers dug into his soft temples, making his head immobile. Needles penetrated his brain leaving his limbs heavy – etherised. The darkness, like an energy, poked his eyes and stifled his breathing.

After careful concentration he made out distinct noises – perhaps his own breath or that of another presence in the room watching him. He wanted to keep his eyes open, but a gas in the air made them weep and close up. Someone else inhabited the room. They slowly approached and murmured – something cruel, degrading. The presence leaned right over him. He felt hot breath; the stink of sweat; the whisper in some impious tongue. He wanted to look but couldn't. His eyes were sewn together. He would live forever in darkness: blind. The presence embraced him, crushed him, crumpled and ripped him in half.

Then he sat bolt upright. Light trapped behind blue translucent screens confused him. Now he understood. He'd been imprisoned in a chamber made to look just like his bedroom – a replica – a very clever one. The changes were subtle but he could discern them: screens designed to look like his curtains. The bed was really a stone table; the wardrobe an iron maiden; a coffin of nails they put enemies into – victims who screamed for mercy. The book shelves were filled with grimoires and scrolls of dark and ancient magical runes. Curses and necromancy used in arcane rituals. The room lay not in a house, but deep below the surface, sunk a million miles into the darkest recess of eternity.

Donny laughed in fearful knowledge of his dying soul. They drained away his spirit into nothingness to use his bones and flesh, now controlled by something alien. He remained outside of it – pushed away. Wanting to feel horror and repulsion, he could only admire their intelligence. They didn't ask or negotiate. They neither warned nor explained. Silent laughter rang in an empty mind which knew no spatial limit; no longer locked inside a head or a human frame, but free. And also powerless. He wanted his body back.

Suddenly everything lit up and a figure he recognised entered the pretend room: someone he knew well. But he could be clever too. It was not her. Of course. It just looked like her. The person who used to be someone he loved cradled his empty carcass and spoke gently to it. He wanted to call out, but what would be the point? The door stood open – he might escape. But the figure overpowered him with the vapour again; the sleep dust – he couldn't fight it.

Hazel hated seeing her brother like this and could only pray she was doing the right thing. Being forced to watch him lose his sanity would kill her. Now she could only mop his brow, change and clean his sheets, and make sure he didn't choke on his own vomit. Hazel hoped her brother might quickly improve but each good day proved only the prelude to a relapse. He slept, cried, shouted or moped. Nothing got through to him.

Donny stayed in bed and the images haunted his fevered brain making him want to sink deeper into the mattress, to fuse himself into it until he became part of the very frame. Eventually his senses would fade – his mouth heal over and his sight dim – until only his essence remained to become dust scattered away on the wind.

Each time Hazel found him either delirious and unresponsive or sobbing with an anguish so consuming him it only made her weep in sympathy. She didn't know what to do except be there for him: just sit while he muttered about the unfairness of the world and a vindictive God. But Hazel didn't know who or what to blame. Her warnings and advice had gone unheeded.

Then one night Hazel woke to a noise and found the front door wide open with no sign of Donny.

Transmuting into the echoing darkness, Donny stumbled through streets, avoiding ghostly figures staring at him. He dodged behind hedges and into alleyways carefully observing passers by. Sometimes they passed so closely he considered reaching out to touch them. In the spectral half-light he made his way to a place where the houses thinned out to a stretch of grass and trees. Climbing a tall fence interwoven with a prickly bush, he scrambled over, ignoring the thorns ripping his loose clothing and the spikes gouging his flesh. He felt a burning in his feet when he landed that rose up through his legs. With simian instinct his head darted left then right as he lifted his nose to smell the air.

In the eerie silence his eyes adjusted to the blackness and when he felt ready ran full pelt, dodging trees, feeling grass then grit under his feet. Trees became ghastly deformed creatures reaching to engulf him with their million twisted, writhing arms. Spindly fingers snapped and cracked as he used his strength to escape their clutches, sprinting over the grass again.

Donny stood beneath a large oak tree and peered up into the immense tangle. Through the foliage he saw a part of the moon and a few scattered stars. If he climbed high enough he might touch those heavenly lights, or dive into the vacuum of space and taste oblivion. In the darkling shadows he pulled himself up on to a low branch and kicked his legs over. He stretched to grab another branch, swinging a few times before hauling himself up again. This gave him the confidence to continue his ascent until the dense tangle and greenery would permit him no further.

As Donny studied civilisation below him, colours faded and the shapes became less distinct; as if his final flame flickered, sputtering out. He allowed himself to fall. At first he floated through the clouds – such elation. But then with gathering momentum he panicked. Something stabbed him sharply in the back and his head forcefully smacked a hard surface. The final thump as he hit the cold floor filled him with a livid hatred for the entire universe.

Hazel sat bleary-eyed, devoid of emotion. The police had tried to reassure her but could do little to comfort her. And now her aging parents were on their way, driving through the darkness to come and help. How would she begin to explain the actions of their son in ways they might understand?

Hazel came to with a jerk as the door slammed and she heard loud, broken breathing in the hallway. An emerging anger was allayed by her sense of relief.

She got up and faced him in the doorway. "Oh my God, what have you done?"

Donny's face was covered in clumps of matted blood and grass. His t-shirt was caked with an amalgam of mud and dried blood from a large cut across his forehead still bleeding. His hands were black with the skin shredded and raw. He stood vacantly staring beyond her.

"Why didn't I die?" he mumbled. He spoke with difficulty as she noticed how swollen his lips were – cut and blistered.

"What do you mean, Don?" Hazel trembled.

"I can't even die properly," he spoke slowly between gulps. "I fell and I wanted to die …" This last word became a sobbing – a rapid fire of staccato gasps whilst his face screwed up into a mask of bestial agony.

She wept silently – forcing herself to believe this would soon be over. How she hated her brother's half-witted cravings. She wanted to blame someone for all this. Yet however much she hated what he did, she loved him.

He fell heavily into her arms as she clutched him firmly and hung on to him for dear life.

And then one wondrous night she hears the voice of her lover calling on the wind. She creeps into the night, enraptured by the hardness of the grass on her bare feet. The cold breeze tingles her skin through her thin nightdress. She wants to merge with nature: be the rejuvenating rain falling upon the earth; the fire that devours with a raging lust; the adamantine rock which endures with a spirit never-ending; the libertine, invisible air that flits and gusts so wantonly. She desires to lie with her love and know his contentment. Then she reaches the forest where the leaves flow silver with moondrops.

A tantalising sensation fills her with longing. With a soft rustling, a figure emerges from the greenwood: a beautiful naked man with copper-coloured hair. His skin glows mottled silver, covered in tiny veins. His limbs are strong and wiry and when he moves a barely perceptible sound makes her shudder.

Beneath the lushness of his graceful arms she becomes comfortably entangled, invisible to the outside world. As she enters his outstretched arms the wisdom and meditation of many centuries overwhelms her mind as she dissolves into his heartwood. And lying down she understands the aching slowness of fulfilment within the timelessness of aeons. Their silence is an eternity – not an emptiness – a pause of serene quietude.

In the darkness she memorises every inch of his silvery grey body; each glossy oval leaf raised up in celebration of life from those strong, slim boughs. Tendrils brush her nakedness with a tenderness never felt before.

Where she touches the strangely warm bark she feels her flesh fusing to the trunk, as if she is the scion being grafted onto the bole. Her limbs become ligneous: hard-grained and static. She finally understands the tentative pleasure of being in harmony with the languid rhythm of nature. She hears the adagio of patient fulfilment lasting for millennia. Now part of the tree – part of creation – she feels joyful in her completeness: a glimpse of the infinite, she has found her place within it.

The delicate fronds of her lover gently caress her.

BRED IN THE BONE

I can't complain about my childhood. I had everything a kid could require: toys, my own room, food, a regular routine and I could watch the TV as much as I wanted. The only thing I felt some regret about was my parents being too strict about me seeing friends, but they had their reasons and I understood them too.

To be honest I didn't have many friends anyway, only Robbo at school and we got into some trouble together, although I was scared of doing anything too bad as it only upset my parents and you don't want to know my Dad when he's angry. Me and Robbo were never bullies or anything like that, just a bit naughty – you know; lazy, not bothering to do the work properly, losing books, giggling and chatting – the sort of things that really irritate teachers, but never get you into serious trouble. We bunked as well, but were clever about it and could expertly forge absence notes. Our form tutor never seemed unduly bothered. I never told my teachers anything, I just kept quiet at school and everyone left me to get on with my own things.

After each day at school, I'd walk home, as it's only a couple of miles, and go to the chip shop for our regular family order. I usually got home about five and I'd have to tidy up the place – usually the mess left by my Dad – feed the dog, a bull terrier called Trooper, and then when Mum came home at six she'd stick the dinner in the microwave and I'd go and wake up Dad.

Dad could be a bit unpredictable at times, but mum was expert at soothing him and they've always been affectionate, so I've got used to them kissing and cuddling in front of me. Mum always asked about school and I'd tell her lies about what I'd learnt which kept her happy.

Dad would always show me his models: he called himself an artist, although he'd never displayed his work and refused to lower himself by joining the commercialised art-world, as it's so full of 'rich bastards who wouldn't understand art if it was crammed up their arseholes'. Dad always made me laugh and we did a lot together. We liked movies and he'd let me stay up into the small hours, even on school nights, watching his favourite films. I've got lots of happy memories of times with Dad.

Dad made my favourite toy: a doll – a strange-looking creature that had no name, but that I had always loved and kept in my bed. It might seem a bit strange for a boy to have a doll, but it was just a toy creature – anyway I loved him the best. Dad was really generous in his art and he'd always be making me things and working out what I'd like next. He was considerate and thoughtful like that.

Sometimes I'd get a bit bored and wish I had a brother or sister, or that I could go out more with Robbo, but Mum and Dad were good company and I understood that I was needed to help them out with things around the house. Honestly I didn't mind. It sounds weird, but I did all the cleaning, cooking and washing, not because they made me, but I knew that they were busy and I had the time to do these things. I was proud to be able to help my parents in this way. I never complained.

Then one day Dad told me he and Mum were going away for a few days, which they had already done a number of times. I'm not scared of being alone; in fact, I'm pretty used to it now and enjoy my own company because I'm used to fending for myself and I'm the most domesticated individual in the house anyway. Looking after Trooper was a bit annoying as he could be quite aggressive and I hated taking him for walks as he would always attack any other dog we met, and even once bit a man who kicked him. Dad was furious and even though the man's leg was bleeding, he said he'd sue the man for kicking his dog. Nothing ever came of it.

With my parents out of the way, I decided to do something I'd never done before. I went home with Robbo after school. I'd never actually been to a friend's house before. Mum and Dad don't really have any friends as they say each other is enough for them, which is quite sweet when you think about it. They don't go out much either, except for work purposes or when they disappear, as they do, for a few nights. So I went home with Robbo and was amazed to see how clean and tidy his house was. There were carpets that looked brand new and he had comfortable chairs and a sofa. It was the first time I had sat on a sofa and I marvelled at the way it curved to your back and felt so soft, softer than my lumpy mattress that was so damp and full of bed bugs. The walls had coloured paper over its smooth, flat surface and held shelves full of books or had paintings framed and tacked to the wall. It was all so new and exciting to my eyes, that people could live like this.

The whole house was so strange and fantastic, but I think I managed to keep my amazement hidden as I had practised so often before. I could conceal the deepest emotions and was proud of my great skill of deception. Perhaps one day I shall be an actor. What struck me most about the house was its overly hygienic cleanliness. His father was polite and shook my hand and his mother, after kissing him, asked me if I wanted to stay for tea. I nodded my head and smiled politely.

Just as I was about to suggest to Robbo that we go out to the park for a bit, his father came in and told him to settle down to his homework to which Robbo dutifully agreed and told me to do the same. This wasn't my idea of fun – I never did my homework, certainly not at home. When it was tea-time I followed Robbo into the bathroom, wandering what he was doing and copied him when he washed his hands, wondering at this odd ritual. What was even weirder was that we all sat down together at a table and had to say a prayer before eating, even though Robbo had never shown any previous signs of being religious.

And then there was the food. It looked colourful, it seemed to be meat, vegetables and gravy – even though I desperately wanted fish and chips. The meat was okay, but a bit chewy and I managed to swallow a few of the vegetables without gagging. Bloody vegetables – I can't stand them and we never eat them anyway – I understand why now. Then we had an apple pie that scorched the inside of my mouth it was so hot and by the end of the meal I thanked Robbo's parents in my politest voice, willing my friend to release me from this godawful situation. Their idea of fun was to sit round a table together and discuss topics that are frankly very dull and pointless. How glad I was that Mum and Dad didn't torture me this way. Robbo also had a younger brother who made rude remarks and I kept thinking that if he was my brother, then my Dad would have given him a good hiding by now and taught him to keep his mouth shut. I probably would punch him in the face if he talked to me like that.

The rest of the evening didn't go too well either, as I was amazed to find out that my friend wasn't even allowed to watch films with a 15 certificate, let alone the sort my Dad let me watch. When Robbo was ordered to bed at nine and told to say goodbye to me, I left with a feeling of relief that my own home life wasn't like this. In fact, it surprised me Robbo was as normal as he was with such tyrannical parents – although I was shocked when he told me his father had never so much as hit him. The colours of the house stayed in my head for a while: the curtains, wallpaper, flowers in vases, the food and Robbo's games and toys, as I strolled home via the off-licence.

I made the stupid mistake of telling Mum I'd been round to Robbo's house, hoping to make her laugh with my description of his weird house. I didn't know she'd tell Dad and he went mental. It was no use trying to explain to him. He clipped me round the ear a few times and that was painful and even when I tried to defend myself like he'd shown me to he still thumped his fist viciously right into my solar plexus, winding me and making me keel over into a foetus shape. Still not sure if he was angry or if this was just one of our play-fights, he grabbed my wrists and lifted me bodily by one hand so that I hung helplessly in front of him and he punched me again in the stomach. I'll admit that I blacked out and came round in the kitchen, to the sight of my Mum ticking me off and telling me that I should do what's good for me. It was a fair point and I eventually got up off the floor, which I realised now was very dirty, and made Dad a cup of tea. I told you, didn't I? Don't mess with my Dad. In any fight situation my Dad's the champ – you've got to hand it to him. He's in his forties now and I'm not exactly small. I'm really proud of him.

I didn't expect it then, but Dad grabbed my hair and I have to admit I flinched – call me a coward, yeah, yeah – but he didn't continue the fight, instead he told me to bring Robbo round. At first I argued but he had a very determined look in his eyes, so I kept quiet, like I've learnt to. I'd never brought anyone round before in my life, but it was a reasonable request and Mum even got out the hoover, wanting to make a good impression.

So after an extremely dull day at school I walked up our street with a friend by my side to our semi-detached house, number 27, and even before I opened the door I could hear Trooper barking gruffly and growling. You need three keys to get into our house as Dad's really tight on security, and I let Robbo go in first and he stood there astounded so I had to give him a push to get him in and close the door. I heard him muttering something about the dirt and the stains on the walls, where there were walls as most of them had either caved in or had holes where things were kept in storage. I could see his eyes become horrified but fascinated by the dead rats in the corner of the hall and the cockroaches that freely scuttled about on the damaged floorboards. I wrestled with Trooper, eventually shutting him in the cupboard under the stairs, where he whined pathetically.

We had no furniture of any note but the floors were littered with newspaper, burger cartons and general detritus now stuck and moulded over the years. It was my home and I was proud of it. I took him to the back room, which had boarded up windows and a naked bulb that made the room glow with a sickly orange mood. My Dad was in there watching a porn film. Robbo was shaking and too timid to speak as I roughly shoved him into the room. My Dad told him to sit on an upturned bucket, which he did with his eyes wide – exactly like Trooper always looks just before my Dad smacks him.

Dad's an imposing figure if you haven't met him. He's not that tall, but he's very wide and stocky, with iron-grey hair and little John Lennon glasses. Wearing only a crumpled t-shirt and boxers, he smiled at me, winked and told me to make a cup of tea. I'm still not sure what happened as I was out making the tea but when I returned with the drinks made, the two were laughing together. I let out Trooper who continued growling and scratching at me, only shutting up when I gave him some of his smelly biscuits, which he wolfed down as he probably hadn't been fed that day.

I beckoned to Robbo, who had to tear himself away from the film that graphically portrayed whatever fetish Dad was into then, and we went upstairs. By now, Robbo was staring wide-eyed and sweating nervously; making comments about wanting to go home, but I called him a chicken and he went sulkily quiet, but at least he stopped whingeing. He looked slightly relieved when we got to my room because it was neater than the rest of the house and I had a television and stereo. He wasn't sure about the mattress in the corner and couldn't believe it was my bed. When he asked me where my duvet was I sniggered scornfully and felt a little sorry for him.

The sound of voices outside my room disturbed us and I looked up to see my Mum come out of her own room with a customer. She just wore a thin negligee and popped her head round the corner to say hi. Robbo's eyes narrowed with confusion, but I felt no need to explain. He was looking at her nipples, I could tell.

Instead I showed him my pride and joy: my toy made for me by Dad. Robbo took it in his hands and turned it over, his face becoming more perplexed like he could almost recognise something. The doll was an obscure figure; its limbs were misshapen and vaguely familiar. My friend took a strand of the doll's hair between his fingers and looked up at me.

"Human hair," I told him casually. His face contorted into a look of disapproval, so I told him the rest. "The body's made up of bones, fingers mainly. It's very clever isn't it? The way it almost looks normal. Dad made it."

"Fucking weird," he whispered. "You're family is fucking weird." He got up very decisively and said with a whimper, "I'm going home now."

That was when I started to feel a bit sad and regretful, because he had always been such a good friend to me, but, after all, as Dad always says, "People never stay friends forever". Good things must always come to an end. The punch I took at him cracked his jaw bone. Clutching it pathetically, Robbo got up and scampered downstairs.

Of course he couldn't open our specially adapted front door and once Dad had bound his mouth with gaffer tape he had become a limp victim and plaything for my parents. Dad didn't make me watch this time, for which I was grateful, so I turned on *The Weakest Link* instead and dialled for a pizza.

The rest was so much easier than you can imagine. I just had to tell the police that the two of us were walking alone when a gang attacked us and Dad even went to the trouble of beating me up a little to provide extra evidence with my new bruises to show me as a fellow victim. Nobody saw Robbo come into our house either – who would? Who the hell knows what their neighbours are up to?

The body parts were discovered ten miles away in a ditch and it made me laugh when I heard that the police are still searching for a violent gang of youths – I told you Dad's bloody clever at this sort of thing. No-one's going to catch my old man. He's the best.

At 4.33 Jerry opened the door to Wayno. Outside he saw a group of half a dozen people walk away. He felt a thrill of fear mixed with the excitement of danger. It felt like he'd taken a dose of extra strong caffeine. There was no way of knowing how this would pan out.

"Brought your gang then?" Jerry said with a nervous smile.

"They're going. I'm on my own now. Just you and me."

Jerry said nothing but held his composure which took a great deal of effort.

"One thing I have to say about you, four-eyes, is you got balls." Wayno growled in a Clint Eastwood-type drawl.

Jerry buzzed with the thrill of the adrenalin rush. It was a kind of compliment – in fact the nicest thing Wayno had ever said to him.

"Why don't you come in?" He held open the door and gestured inside.

Wayno stayed on the threshold craning his neck round to try and see inside.

"Is this some kind of trap? You got all your teacher buddies in there or something?"

"No-one. I'm the only person here," he replied. "Would you like a cup of tea?"

"Nah, you can't get pissed on that" He strutted past Jerry and went into the living room, checking everything out as if casing the joint. "Got any booze, man?"

"You know," Wayno said as he admired the plasma television, "grassing me up like that wasn't very nice. I think you need to apologise."

This wasn't quite how he'd planned the visit. Somehow he'd naively expected the bully to be more compliant.

"You know what? You're right." Jerry tried to stick to the plan. "It was a stupid thing to do and I am genuinely sorry."

Wayno appeared taken aback by this. "Hope you get punished then. Otherwise that ain't fair."

"I've got to spend lunchtimes and after school with Mr Platt for the next few weeks," Jerry explained truthfully.

Wayno smirked and let out a whispery hiss just like a snake might make if it laughed. "Old Pratty. What a complete joke he is. Not exactly a scary punishment – what's he going to do? Bore you to death?"

As the two boys laughed together Jerry wondered what on earth was going on. It seemed to be going too well but he stayed on guard for any unpredictable turn, which was just as well, because Wayno looked equally uncomfortable.

"Look here Goggles. I'm not your mate, you know. I don't forgive that easily. In fact, I still feel like I want rip out your spinal column."

Jerry stood there stupidly with no idea what to do now. If he punched Wayno he would be murdered in cold blood. He had to stay calm. Stick to the script.

Jerry grinned and shook his head slowly.

"Let's make this fair shall we?" he said.

"Huh?"

"I take my glasses off and you remove your contact lenses."

Discomfort registered itself immediately in Wayno's face in the form of a slight twitch.

"How d'you know that?"

"I know more than you think. You see we have quite a lot in common, you and me."

"I ain't no four-eyed freak like you."

"Oh," Jerry replied whilst pulling a face. "Then tell me what that writing says on the side of that bag next to the shed ... without your contacts." He pointed out the window. "You can't can you? Nor can I if I take my glasses off. So let's make this fair."

Jerry made a big mime of taking off his glasses and putting them in their case and placing them on the table. "Or are you scared?"

Wayno stared dumbly, stunned with his mouth wide-open, catching flies.

Jerry felt the adrenalin pumping through every vein and corpuscle.

It worked. Wayno took out a small plastic container, fished out his lenses with his little finger, which he deposited carefully in the container, then replaced it into his pocket. Wayno looked less confident now.

"Do you know what? I'm not in the least bit scared of you," Jerry continued. "I actually feel sorry for you. Thank God I'm not like you. And you call me a freak?"

Wayno's lips began to quiver as an energy began to stir inside him. One side of his face tightened, moving swiftly down both arms to his fingers that flexed with a tingling sensation. Then it affected his legs which bent into a springing position after which he leapt from his feet towards Jerry.

Expecting to feel a sharp pain Jerry jerked his body to one side only to watch Wayno shoot past uncontrollably into the sofa. Wayno got up and swung his head around confused and angry before crouching in some kind of martial arts pose. Jerry made for the back door.

"Oi, Cadman," Jerry called with some nerve. "Out here." Scrambling with the key he got the door open and as calmly as he could he stepped outside and stood visibly in the middle of the lawn, bracing himself. His back garden sat snugly surrounded by a tall evergreen hedge and backed onto a little copse which gave them a great deal of privacy from any prying neighbours.

"You little git. I'm gonna rip your bloody head off …"

"Yeah, yeah," Jerry said in a bored tone. "You said that before. Didn't happen though did it?"

For once Wayno looked a little taken-aback – probably not used to his victims standing up for themselves, thought Jerry.

"Not so tough now, eh?" Jerry taunted, quickly checking everything was in position.

This caused another charge.

Jerry's pulse raced to dangerous levels, but in that split-second he felt a warm hazy mist around him and then relaxed into its embracing grip.

What happened next amazed Jerry considerably. He laughed as he watched Wayno leap at him in what seemed like slow motion. Now only a few inches away from each other Jerry could study the boy's angry demeanour in some detail. First he saw bloodshot eyes with black bags above pock-marked, sunken cheeks. The mouth which was always twisted down now opened in a scowl; spittle gathering in the thin corners of his pale lips.

With some amusement Jerry watched as Wayno pulled back a fist, knuckles white with intensity. The fist then began its slow journey towards his own face and Jerry felt confident enough to wait until it came within a few inches before he calmly leaned to one side and watched the fist waft uselessly past him. The momentum of the failed punch was enough to cause Wayno to lose his balance. The boy stumbled forwards, his legs tangling with Jerry's. But as he looked on, Wayno slowly spread his arms and Jerry worked out that Wayno was attempting to grab his legs. Instead Jerry stepped out of the looping arms before they could enclose him and he watched the bully hit his head on a piece of crazy paving. The whole incident made Jerry feel powerful – like some invincible warrior.

Suddenly everything returned to normal speed as Wayno lay in a crumpled heap, holding his back in agony. Jerry almost felt sorry for him and felt willing to shake hands and let him go. But the bully had other ideas.

Standing up, Wayno rolled his head round a few times, his neck cracking at various intervals. He rotated both shoulders which also made gristly noises and with eyes almost popping from his head faced the enemy once more.

"I'm gonna kill ya!"

Jerry smiled. Now was the time for his plan to come into action. He hoped he'd wound up Wayno enough for this to work.

Jerry scrambled up the ladder, positioned to take him onto the roof of his house. Once on the red slates he took a breath and waited for Wayno's next move.

Jerry became aware of a much cooler breeze with no shelter at this height. Wayno looked up and gripped the bottom of the ladder.

"Come and get me you short-sighted fairy!" How Jerry enjoyed saying that line.

With an expression of uncertainty Wayno began a slow ascent, gripping the ladder tightly and keeping his body close to the metallic rungs.

Eventually Wayno got to the top and Jerry could see fear in his face. The boy refused to move his head which remained fixed ahead, with eyes bulging and streaming.

"Come and get me Cadman," Jerry hissed. "Unless you're too scared."

Wayno shook himself and made the final push over the top of the ladder and onto the sloping red slates of the house roof towards his quarry. Jerry had to remain guarded and in control of himself now, even more so than before.

Shuffling slowly up towards him, Wayno slipped slightly and without a thought landed on his backside and froze in a seated position.

"I gotta get down," Wayno whimpered. "Need to get down. Please help me."

"The chimney's right behind you," Jerry suggested amicably. "Shuffle up on your bum, but mind any loose slates or you'll fall to your death." Jerry had to suppress a snort of laughter as he said this.

Painfully slowly, Wayno inched his way backwards up towards the chimney, holding out one hand which, finally, wrapped itself gratefully around the squared corners. Wayno gasped with relief as he hauled himself behind the chimney stack, with his back against the black and orange brickwork. His breathing became shallow and hoarse.

"Not so big and scary now are you?"

Wayno concentrated on his breathing, gulping noisily and hugging himself.

"I thought you were going to rip my head off or something?" Jerry allowed himself a smirk. "It's an incredible view," he continued. "Come over here and have a look."

Wayno shook his head and continued hugging his knees.

"Oh no, I've just remembered – you're short-sighted. You can't see all that way, can you?"

Jerry stepped carefully towards him.

"Would you like me to help you get down?"

Wayno looked up with the face of a little child and nodded helplessly.

This was an opportunity for some kind of negotiation, so Jerry thought hard about his next words.

"I want you to remember this moment the next time you see me."

Wayno nodded his head vigorously, pressing himself so fervently back into the chimney, that it wouldn't have surprised Jerry if he turned into one of those stone gargoyles the same colour as the bricks. His facial expression was grotesque enough. It was then Jerry heard Wayno stammering – in genuine fear.

He almost felt sorry for Wayno now and put the final part of his plan into action.

"Take my hand and I'll get you down safely."

Wayno blubbered something inaudible.

"Oh for God's sake, don't be such a baby or else I'll tell everyone at school what a scaredy-cat cry-baby you are. Look I want you off my soddin' roof and if you want the same then you'll have to trust me."

Eventually he took Jerry's hand and slowly shuffled along the very top ridge of the roof on all fours.

"Stand up, Wayne."

"I c-c-can't."

"Stand up now," Jerry commanded.

Wayno closed his eyes and rose up carefully until he stood straight. He put both arms on Jerry's shoulder as if in affectionate embrace.

"Open your eyes." Jerry waited until his order was obeyed. "I promise you we'll both get down safely if you do as I tell you."

Smiling nonchalantly, Jerry enjoyed the moment when he finally had power over this boy who'd caused him so much stress and grief for so long. The change in status felt good. Wayno's arm began to tighten around his neck and throat.

"I didn't know you cared. Look I'm really flattered but I don't feel the same about you." Jerry sniggered, elated.

But Wayno neither laughed nor let go.

Now for the dangerous bit, thought Jerry. With Wayno wrapped around him, Jerry could just reach the rope and harness attached to their giant oak tree. The rope had been there all along in view, but Wayno had not seen it. In a well-practiced move Jerry pulled the rope tight and carefully attached it to the harness on his belt. He tested how secure it felt and remembered the exhilaration of the few practice-runs he had attempted before this moment.

"No sudden movements, Wayne." Jerry sidestepped then grabbed hold of the boy with all his might. He had to get this right. Looking down towards the lawn all Jerry could see in his short-sightedness was a swirling, hazy mist before him.

"Hold on tight!" he called into Wayno's ear. "We're going down!"

Wayno turned to look at Jerry and his face streamed with tears – confused and pitiful. Jerry twisted Wayno's head round, forcing him to watch the next bit.

Then Jerry crouched, took a few quick steps and flung himself and his passenger off the sloping tiles. Wayno shrieked like a banshee, kicking his feet against Jerry's shins whilst his arms swung wildly like broken windmills.

"Help me! Oh God, no. I don't want to die!" Wayno screamed in a high pitch squeal.

The two boys tipped with a jerking frenzy over the guttering and plummeted towards the back garden with a terrific velocity – rushing towards the garden. Then within inches of smashing into the floor they came to a sudden halt and just floated there upside down. Wayno, now wheezing for breath in an asthma attack, went limp in Jerry's arms. Jerry dropped Wayno the last few feet. His nemesis lay on the grass below him, either unconscious or paralysed with fear.

After a few minutes Wayno shook his head clear, looked up at Jerry magically floating above him, glanced around for a point of escape; noticed the back door still open and scarpered through it, into the hallway and out of the front door.

Jerry released his harness and did a commando roll onto the lawn.

He lay on the grass for a long time; exhilarated and terrified.

He tried to imagine the whole episode from Wayno's perspective and more he thought he more he laughed until the laughing hurt too much.

Before his parents returned he had to put away the ladder and return his dad's tree surgery equipment to the shed.

Once inside and after a chance to get back his breath, Jerry attempted to still the images racing through his mind, and could only wish that now life might start going back to normal again.

DIONYSUS

As if delivered by a lightning flash, he appears: famous, beautiful and seemingly immortal … capturing the souls of a whole generation like moths in a net.

The worshippers chant their ritual, genuflecting before the altar. A discordant hum of anticipation becomes the intonation of an arcane creed: to see Him in the flesh, hear the voice, be hypnotised by those gestures and taste the energy – to finally transcend. Some come to be healed, some to be inspired; others to escape their own loneliness. For many He remains their only link with reality and tonight they will find life and sacred purpose, before returning to the hopeless anonymity of their insignificant lives. But this night brings catharsis and fulfilment. They wait expectantly at his shrine – a horde moving as one organism.

Mrs McDermott walked in to her daughter's bedroom. In the darkness she could see the walls covered from ceiling to floor with photo posters of him – most of them practically naked. She stopped when she saw a life-size cardboard cut-out. Underneath, the words "Fuck the System" stood out harshly as he gazed into her soul with his livid cerulean eyes.

Then the door flung open and the light came on, making Mrs McDermott jump. She hadn't heard the front door open.

"Who said you could come in here?"

Under her wild purple hair, heavy Gothic make-up hid Emma's freckles, emphasising instead her eyes and lips. She wore a short leather skirt and a white crop-top with a plunging neckline vividly revealing her red frilly bra. Emma's high-heeled sling-backs made her totter precariously.

"I'm going to bed. Are you just going to stand there?"

Mrs McDermott checked her watch again. 3.37 am.

As the lights dim, a profound silence reigns: an eerie electric tension. Shadows move in the gloaming as each individual joins in the irresistible incantation, "Dionysus! Dionysus!" All eyes strain to pick up a slight movement through the dry ice spurting on stage as a figure appears. A rapid scream of guitar scales sings out into the night as thousands of devotees shout in veneration to the avatar now visible in a spectral glow; there He stands – the apotheosis of a million dreams. His eldritch features are handsome and arrogant, with a body strong and lithe like a dancer. Barefoot and with unkempt hair he wears only cut jeans, showing off his perfect torso; his arms encircled with golden filigree bands.

"Come on, Embo!" Mr McDermott called from the bottom of the stairs. "Did you hear me, you little scamp? I'm coming to get you." Bounding up alternate steps he opened her door and peered into the darkness.

"We'll be late, Emmylou," he called to her. After a discernible movement, a dark head emerged from the duvet. The voice sounded hoarse and edgy.

"Go away."

Mr McDermott's intuition told him to laugh. He moved toward the bed. "Come on, poppet, you've still got time."

"I'm not bloody going." Emma's voice became harsher and more determined.

Mr McDermott grabbed the bottom of the duvet and snatched it off the bed. To his utter shock she lay stark naked on the mangled bed sheet. He stood there speechless.

"Piss off, dad," she spat, as she lay there unselfconsciously exposed. Mr McDermott looked away quickly.

Shaken and confused, he left her alone.

The guitar crashes into a thumping, familiar riff as the bassist follows with two huge chords signalling the introduction to 'Sexual Exorcism'. Thousands of voices sing the opening lyric, "From gentle seduction to eager temptation ..." Dionysus doesn't bother to start the song; no need when adoring fans will do it for you and pay for the privilege. Eventually, he joins in and the crowd listen to their hero.

> *And love exists behind your screams*
> *As I enact erotic dreams.*
> *I'm touching you explicitly,*
> *To exorcise you sexually!*

"What can we do to stop her?" Mrs McDermott couldn't help weeping. "She's changed so much – I just can't understand what's happening."

"I know," her husband replied as he comforted his wife.

"It's that concert. That ... man – what's he called? Dionysus? She's got pictures everywhere."

"That bloody concert. We should've been stricter and stopped her going. We're too soft on her. You've always been soft, spoiling her and letting her go out at all hours."

His words hurt deeply, but she had no energy to argue.

"She certainly won't be going again." Mr McDermott slammed his hand on the table and moved over to his desk to switch on his laptop.

Emma screamed and danced, forcing her way to the front so she could reach the stage and once there she stood with her arms out begging. If only he would touch her, then she would know it to be a sign. She pleaded and implored with her eyes; stretched her fingers as far as they would reach; she screamed the words not caring about the tune. At the end of the song, the singer walked up to the surging crowd and gave one fan a high five and then let his fingers run along the outstretched hands like a boy knocking a fence as he passes by. Emma felt his light touch on her own fingertips knowing that when he sang the next song he would sing it for her.

Dionysus' voice hits the final note with a perfectly pitched screech and holds the note longer than anyone else in the arena. The wild applause drowns out the beginning of the guitar solo in which Dionysus' fingers glide and flick with supernatural dexterity sending the crowd into paroxysms of delight. His guitar is a magic amulet of paranormal power perfecting subtle changes and intricacies, twisting and turning through impossible sequences, with the sound of a demented banshee.

She knew she must have him. Before leaving the stage Dionysus looked into her eyes; she felt him gaze deeply into her very soul. She had made herself beautiful for him and one touch was not enough. Her aching grew more frantic. She must get backstage and do anything to meet him face to face.

Desperate to show their adoration, they mimic the bewitching gestures of Dionysus and share his every mood and feeling, from passionate to the hauntingly melancholic.

Then the well-known anthem – the latest hit single – called 'Law of Chaos' begins with a sudden explosion of sound and keeps up a manic tempo of sustained punk-like aggression.

> *Faces licked by tongues of serpents*
> *Bacchae dancing in the dust,*
> *Galloping in hungry madness*
> *Gorging on the wine of lust.*

"Yeah, I can introduce you to him," said the fat security guard. "I'll get you into the after show party. You stick with me."

Thrilled to find it so easy, Emma shook with anticipation and followed him through the doors marked 'Strictly no access to the public'.

The crowd willingly succumb to the chaos and madness of the music – laughing and weeping in ecstasy. 'Fuck the System', had become the anthem of its age. It broke all previous sales records as soon as it was banned and then stayed at number one in the charts for more than four months.

> *Some blame the churches, others the schools*
> *But I blame politicians – they're all fools!*

His voice sneers and snarls as thousands of fists pound the air.

The security guard tore her blouse, pushing her down on the hard, cold floor. She panicked as she saw him undo his trousers under his big, hairy belly, and then felt his stony fingers clamp between her legs. As he puffed and grunted she felt an agonising pain as he pulled her head right back by the hair. But she realised this was how it must be. She must suffer for Him: gradually work her way to her goal – and soon she would be with Him.

Drums crash maniacally as a rhythm for the mass of black swaying leather and whipping hair. Dionysus sings the verse to the accompaniment of simple bass chords, before developing into the fury of the chorus with its violent imagery of 'mind-fucked automata'. As his votaries sing the chorus line over and over Dionysus lets rip with a guitar break which sears through every heart, as if possessed. His fingers run up and down the fret board effortlessly creating a sinewy mesh of music.

"Fuck the System! My music is the life-force – drink deep of my music."

As the crowd scream desperate pleads, beseeching him to remain with them, Dionysus spins away with an arrogant smirk and leaves them to fight amongst themselves.

The fat man shuddered as if in pain, slobbering over her face, and she closed her eyes and imagined Him touching her. He was her lover, teaching and guiding her. She would bend to his every need and he would always be there to lead her deeper and further into His mysteries.

"Where do you think you're going, young lady?"

"Out. What's it got to do with you?" Emma had never spoken to him like this before. What had happened to his little girl?

"Don't you dare talk to me like that."

"I'm going out and you ain't gonna stop me."

He grabbed her arm and squeezed hard.

"Stop right where you are," he shouted, but as she struggled in his grip her sleeve ripped and she stared at him with malice. Mr McDermott was shaken.

"Fuck off. Fuck you and fuck everybody else. This is my life and I'll fucking well do whatever I fucking like!"

Without thinking he slapped her. She pushed him away with a

terrific force and swept out of the house. The slamming door made the house shake to its foundations. Mr McDermott felt more scared than he'd ever been in his life.

Chugging bass then formed a new layer of sound, chanted by a thousand voices:

> *Because you know you'll never rest*
> *'Til you confess, confess…*
> *You'll never pass the test*
> *And your life will be a mess*
> *'Til you confess.*

A pretty teenage girl with purple hair and gothic make-up was ushered on to the stage. The singer touched her with his hands, his guitar and even with his tongue. She gyrated slowly as he caressed her slim, young body. Then she bent over for Dionysus to simulate the sexual act. The singer slowly undressed her and she showed no resistance. Lascivious snarls erupted from the men at the foot of the stage. Hands desperately clawed the air in a palpable form of frustrated energy. The now naked girl knew how to tease them, confidently using her body to arouse each hot-blooded male.

Mr McDermott pressed his thumb and forefinger into the corner of his eyes. All this internet research made his eyes sore. His laptop had revealed pornographic pictures of Dionysus: lyrics of his songs banned worldwide by all major stations; bills and amendments from various parliaments and councils attempting to restrict the influence he seemed to have. After trawling through fansites, webzines and galleries dedicated to this enigma he knew he'd read enough, having found the information he'd been looking for. Grabbing his mobile, wallet and keys, he slipped out of the house.

The recognisable bass and drum intro signalled the beginning of their twenty-minute epic – 'Burnt Offerings'. The first part of the song, called 'Penance', sprung to life as a furious and brutal thrash anthem that segued into part two: 'Atonement'. This section calmed the mood down; its elegant, atmospheric keyboards became a hypnotic tone as the crowd swayed in unison with the words 'reparation' and 'expiation' repeated like a mantra. The mood suddenly changed to one of mysticism. Dionysus, without warning, crashed through this gentle soft mood with a searing crescendo that raised the pulses and the adrenaline levels of the crowd. It created a form of hysteria. People leapt, shook, howled, punched and convulsed their bodies and heads as if walking through flames or dying in violent fits. The finale to the song, 'Salvation', contained irresistible hook-lines and a sing-along chorus.

> *Full of anger, full of pain*
> *An ancient power will rise again.*
> *Where you stand is sacred ground*
> *But no salvation can be found...*
> *No salvation ...No redemption*

The final words kept being repeated with the second syllable elongated in each.

As the band reached the climax of the song, lasers and strobe lighting added to the general feeling of ecstasy. The fans continued chanting 'No salva-a-a-tion ... No rede-e-e-emption...'.

He felt horribly out of place amidst the mass of leather and thrashing arms, especially in his expensive suit. The music was horrifically loud to his ears and he regretted coming. Pushing roughly through the crowd he peered with narrowed eyes at the figures on stage. When full realisation hit him he was startled into a slowly rising panic.

Dionysus screamed for his followers to do his bidding. Emma knew with a mounting and absolute conviction that the words were meant for her. Her body no longer her own, she allowed herself to be taken. External, alien thoughts and images flushed through her mind, displacing all memories and self-awareness. To be at one with Him was her only desire.

"You love me and want me ... now come to me ... inside me ... and live your perfect dream."

A man she thought she recognised stood below her. He gestured and pleaded to her. For the sake of Dionysus she went to this man. In obedience she would serve her Master. Emma descended into the crowd, moving easily through it, as if alone in a frozen world. She looked up to the stage and saw Dionysus stare, grin and guide her forwards. As she pressed on the throng gave way to each push.

She felt her heart stirring – responding to words in her head: chants placed there in her unconscious mind. This song was called 'Sacrificial Ritual' – about the necessary punishment of an unbeliever to appease the jealous god. Dionysus now whispered something about vengeance ... insult ... atonement ...

The man saw the girl approaching him. His face expressed anger and then pity. His gestures indicated sorrow and became a semaphore of pleading. When he tried to shout he knew his words would not reach her.

Emma strode towards the suited man's awkwardly balanced body – motionless and vulnerable. Something almost stopped her – but then she heard his voice once more. To only please him.

"For denying me even though I am God – for that there is no salvation!"

The girl brought up her hand, which gripped a vicious blade. She clasped the victim's hair with the other hand then jerked the head back to reveal the length of his smooth white throat. With a single swipe the girl slit open the soft, naked skin. Then she dropped the dagger which skidded away against a still pair of feet.

Just then, at a gesture from Dionysus, the world sprang back to life and crimson blood spewed from the falling man's neck.

A ghastly whisper echoed through the hall as the crowd became suddenly reanimated.

"No redemption."

The events that follow were caught on cameras and mobile phones, which the news stations managed to piece together to make sense of this sensational, terrifying story. The video clip was uploaded onto the internet and watched by over a billion people.

The film shows a young girl murdering her own father. His collapsed and prone body has blood gushing from his hewn-open neck. Next to him stands his daughter –naked – with a malicious grin contorting her face, clumps of hair in her hands. As the drumming continues, she dances and shrieks in ecstasy. The crowds around her appear confused or stoned, as they begin to sway and slowly turn inwards. Her face suddenly changes to one of terror and confusion as she looks down at her hands. Recognition spreads as she kneels besides the mangled corpse, pulling its head towards her. She mouths a scream and convulses horrifically. Here the camera begins to shake and swing violently until it is clearly dropped and ignored, half-cocked on the floor.

A CCTV camera shows the mob all now focussed on the girl and the prostrate body of her father. The naked girl looks up and seems to welcome the stretched out hands. Her face is serene as she is engulfed by voracious ripping and tearing and biting. The death is fast and vicious. When the baying crowds pull back there are just chunks of raw meat and pieces of limbs scattered over the blood-spattered floor. The dead pair are both unrecognisable and indistinguishable. Ragged tatters of cloth are also strewn in the gory mess. When the police and medical rescue arrive they are met by a hall full of thousands of hysterical people, screaming, shaking and weeping for the end of the world. First-aiders comfort some and wrap them in warm blankets. Others are stretchered off into ambulances.

Television stations receive thousands of complaints after showing the coverage.

Dionysus and his band disappeared, unseen by individual or technology. But his influence increases more than ever. Myths and conspiracy theories appear regularly on the Internet. Movies, TV series and books continue to be commissioned and never seem to quench the world's thirst for their voyeuristic pleasures.

Six months after Dionysus' baffling disappearance, a journalist received an unmarked CD through the post. It contained twelve brand new songs from Dionysus. Each one brilliant: raw, original, provocative and irresistible.

> *I am your god. I am your deity.*
> *Forget your sorrows when you bow down to me.*
> *I am your fate – now I will set you free ...*

The thirteenth track plays as a DVD showing Dionysus' face in a close-up shot – his face painted crimson and his eyes completely black. As he speaks his white tongue protrudes lasciviously. Watching him you have no idea if you are being seduced or mocked. His voice is a velvet bag full of golden serpents.

The stranger walked straight up to her, clearly wanting to talk. Her immediate impression was favourable – good-looking if a bit skinny – so she signalled to her friends to walk on. He spoke first.

"You're a Sagittarius. I can tell by your face."

"Lucky guess," she replied, staring through narrowed eyes, aware of her friends looking back giggling.

"Let me read your palm," he said casually.

"What now? Here?"

"Sure. Why not?"

"I've never met you before and you already want to hold my hand?"

"Can't blame a guy for trying." He kept his eyes steadily on her. "What have you got to lose … except your heart?"

"Corny," she said. He shrugged inside his faded leather jacket and she gazed down at his black Converse Hi-Tops with the laces undone. She had to make a snap decision on whether to humour him or walk on. The attractive contrast between his light blue eyes and black spiky hair convinced her it might be worth a laugh.

"Give me one minute. If you're not impressed walk away," he suggested coolly.

"You sound like a salesman. What are you selling?"

"Myself."

"Pretty confident aren't you?"

He shrugged again and held out his hand. She placed hers on top, the palm facing up.

"Impress me then."

He gently caressed her hand, studying the lines, whorls and veins with great consideration. Then he carefully turned her face towards his and gazed into her eyes, smiling, which she felt animated his eyes. Eventually he spoke, keeping hold of her warm hand.

"You're full of compassion; patient and thoughtful. You want to work with people helping them with their problems. I see an excellent sense of humour; you're intelligent and quick-minded – witty. Socially, you'd rather have a few close friends than a huge crowd of acquaintances. There are times when you feel lonely like no one really understands you. You know you should do more – give something back to society but you're never sure quite what to do." He stopped and looked up. "How am I doing?"

"I agree with everything so far," she said with a nervous chuckle. "All these things are true but they're pretty general. You could be describing anyone. Isn't this technique called cold-reading like mediums use to fish for information?" She felt she'd rumbled him and grew in confidence. His next words surprised her.

"Your name is … wisdom – Sophia. I can see in your face you're wiser than your years. A name fit for a goddess."

"My name is Sophie. But you could have asked someone."

Undeterred the stranger continued looking at her hand.

"You weren't born in this country. Um, let's see ..." His eyes cut into her like lasers. "New Zealand ... but then you moved here as a little child which explains why you don't have a Kiwi accent."

"Have you been reading my personal records? They're confidential, you know."

"Ok then," the stranger said as if accepting a challenge. "You once owned a cat which died on your bed one night. When you woke up the next morning it lay stiff and lifeless on your pillow with a stain of blood round its mouth."

"How the hell could you know that?" Her expression became more uncertain. "Are you some kind of mind-reader?"

"And you were in love with one guy. You had a short passionate affair but it had to end when his wife got pregnant. Unrequited love, eh? The shittiest thing on the planet. It really knocked you: you still think about him, don't you?"

"This is a joke right? Someone's set me up. Where's the camera? Is this some reality TV show? How the hell could you know those things? I never told anybody."

"Would that be because he was your cousin?"

Sophie felt unsettled and her eyes showed confusion. She began to regret sending her friends away. The stranger still smiled kindly.

"This is too weird." Sophie began to look suspiciously at him. "Are you someone on telly? A magician or psychic? What's going on?"

The stranger shuffled and let go of her hand.

"I'm Zeke and you and I are destined to be together."

She snorted and shook her head in disbelief.

"Do you believe in fate?" Zeke continued stubbornly.

"Not really. I'm an atheist – I believe in free-will. I control every part of my own future."

"Liar."

"Well if you're going to be offensive I'll be off."

"But that's bollocks about controlling your future. You didn't have any say in where you were born or who your parents were. You didn't control your dad's future…"

"What the fuck do you know about my Dad?" Sophie moved away but instantly stopped when she felt a hand on her shoulder.

"I just mean that you need to be honest."

"And what makes you think I'm not telling the truth?" Sophie easily wriggled out of the loose grip.

"Because I know you better than you know yourself."

"Dream on, buddy." She began to regret this whole incident. "You have all the lines don't you? Get over yourself."

"You're not an atheist – not religious either, I admit – but maybe agnostic. You've been brought up to believe in God and you struggle with doubts, but there's no way you're an atheist."

Sophie couldn't think clearly. She felt trapped yet intrigued.

"Look, who the hell are you? Why should I trust you?"

"I told you. I'm Zeke and I'm your future."

"You sound like a psycho and I'm getting scared now. I'm going to walk away."

"Isn't love at first sight the essence of the romantic ideal? You should follow your instincts – don't think, just feel and jump in."

She couldn't speak but neither could she walk away.

Zeke smiled. "So you'll go out with me then?"

"Well…"

"We could go out for a meal – somewhere public – bring a chaperone if you're worried. I won't expect anything else; just a meal and a chance for you to get to know me."

Her face expressed a conflict. "Just a meal and a chat?"

"Nothing else. I won't bite … unless you want me to. After that if you're not sure then I promise to leave you alone."

"Why me?"

During the short silence he stared at her intently.

"Please don't freak out but you've got to believe me when I say I'm in love with you. I'm crazy about you."

Sophie's nose and forehead wrinkled as she attempted to understand. Before she could take guard he leaned forward and kissed her on the cheek. A card was thrust into her hand.

"Call me."

And with that he sauntered off.

She didn't phone. Nor did she throw away the number. She told Flo about him and her reaction confirmed her own decision.

"God, he sounds well creepy. Probably another sleazebag who wants to get in your knickers and let's face it, you usually run an open-door policy."

"Piss off you old tart." Sophie wasn't in the mood for being teased.

"Maybe this could be the one you say no to," Flo suggested.

"What so you can shag him? That's all you ever get, eh? My cast-offs."

Jabbering and cackling unselfconsciously, the two friends found their way into the megaplex. The film they saw was a predictable Rom-Com, but did afford them the sight of the male lead's pert buttocks, which they felt made it worth the entrance fee.

After which they walked to the Mexican bar and ordered two white wine spritzers. Turning to find some seats they bumped into someone familiar.

"Oh hiya – it's my goddess of wisdom. You didn't call."

"Correct," she replied bluntly. There he stood, black spiky hair and piercing blue eyes. Sophie began to wonder if this meeting was a coincidence.

"Enjoy the film?"

Zeke obviously saw her expression of panic as he put his hand on her bare arm. "I saw you and your friend going in to the cinema while I was queuing up to go bowling."

An awkward few seconds prevailed.

"Mind if I join you two?" Zeke seemed unaware of Sophie's discomfort.

"What about your friends? The ones you went bowling with."

"They've gone. I was about to go when I saw you."

He sat next to Flo. Sophie sighed and went to buy a round. When she returned she heard Flo being predictably flirty.

"You can have my phone number if you like – as you gave yours away to my friend."

"Flo – put your libido away."

Flo ignored her and nudged Zeke. "Do you know what winks and makes love like a tigress?" Zeke shook his head. Flo leaned closer to him and winked slowly, pouting and making sure he could see down her low-cut top.

"That's it, we're off." Sophie grabbed her coat and started walking towards the exit.

"Do you mind if I come with you?" Zeke asked.

"Looks like you already are," Sophie mumbled.

"Oh don't be like that, Sophe," Zeke insisted. "I'm not interested in Flo. I only have eyes for you."

Flo harrumphed and stomped ahead of them out into the cold evening.

"Why are you so up your own arsehole?" Sophie asked him as they walked. "You seem to assume I fancy you. Do you spend your entire life believing every girl you ever meet wants to jump in bed with you? Flo can have you for all I care."

"I've judged this all wrong haven't I?" Zeke mumbled as much to himself. Sophie let it go. "I'm sorry if I said the wrong thing. I didn't mean to offend you. I'm probably trying too hard."

"I feel like I'm being bullied into something. That's not the way to impress me."

"I just wanted to make a mark."

"Well, you did that all right, although it's more of an unwanted stain at the moment."

They both stopped and laughed together. Sophie's thoughts became positive again and she wondered if she was being paranoid.

Turning the corner Flo waved and disappeared through a gate towards her first floor flat.

"Come on, I'll walk you home," Zeke said, smoothly.

"No, I'm fine – it's not very far from here. You go," Sophie replied.

"No, no, I insist. It's okay, it's on my way."

Sophie stopped in her tracks.

"How do you know?"

"What?" Zeke raised his hands in innocence.

"How do you know where my house is?"

Zeke's blue eyes flicked to either side as his eyebrows furrowed.

"You were doing really well until that point, Zeke – or whatever your name is." Sophie felt angry now. "Have you been stalking me?"

"You couldn't be more wrong…"

"Your behaviour's been bloody weird right from the start and I should've listened to my instinct. You did your best and failed, okay? So get over it and find a new victim."

"But if you'll just give me one more chance…"

"No I don't think you understand. I don't want to see you again. Is that clear enough for you?" Sophie's voice grew angrily intense. "Next time I'll call the police."

To her relief he held up his hands as if she pointed a gun at him and began to move cautiously backwards. No more words were spoken as he turned and loped off into the shadows.

The next evening Sophie slobbed about, watching bad TV. As a child she remembered there being just a few channels of crap, now there seemed to be four hundred. Unpeeling herself finally from her chair she filled a glass with tap water before double-locking the front door. With her two housemates out clubbing, there was no way of knowing whether they'd come home tonight.

Sophie followed her usual routine. She went upstairs to her bedroom to get undressed and to don her white fluffy dressing gown, before descending again with a fresh towel to the shower room: a small space next to the kitchen with a lockable door. She hooked open the small, high window to let out the steam. The hot water soothed her aching bones although she was careful not to wet her hair tonight having tied it up in a top knot. Switching off the spray she pushed the Perspex door open and felt a cold draft.

A movement by the open window startled her. A pair of eyes stared in before the shape disappeared in a flash. Her instinct told her to grab her towel and let its soft comfort embrace her. As she stood on tiptoe to inspect the window a white object moved, making her flinch. Then she saw a large moth clicking noisily as if uncertain whether to come in or not. Pulled in by the light, the moth hovered in the dark gap and as if dangling from a string, made a clumsy entry into the room. It had a fat hairy body and brown, speckled wings. Each with a black spot surrounded by white – just like eyes. Could she have been so mistaken? She could have sworn the eyes had been blue. And had the window been that far open before? Sophie tried to recollect how hard she had pushed it.

Using a flannel to shoo out the moth became a pointless exercise. It was determined to bash against the spotlight mounted into the tiled wall. Instead she dried herself quickly and climbed into her dressing gown, keeping her back to the moth at all times. The idea of being watched by a voyeur – be it human or insect – made her shiver. Flashing her boobs on a roller-coaster camera when drunk was one thing, but being spied on without her knowledge seemed plainly sinister. This way lacked any kind of control on her part – and Sophie hated that.

Over the next few nights, Sophie's mind refused to settle. What else did he know about her? She knew about identity theft but this was going too far. Perhaps he got his information from her friends – or from her Facebook profile. She tried to remember what she'd written on her blog and which photographs were available. Even though her privacy settings were on the highest level she didn't fully trust these social network sites, having read the horror stories. But how did Zeke know about Florry, her cat? Or about her affair with Gareth?

"He's obviously done his homework," she told herself as she looked in the mirror. "I wonder if he's getting inside information."

As she lay awake at night a surprising fantasy formed in her mind. If brutally honest, the thought of being watched secretly actually excited her. That her body had such a strange effect on men never ceased to amaze her. Eyes devouring her and spying on her as she undressed became an irresistible titillation she could not shake off. What surprised her most as she luxuriated further into the depths of her fantasies, was the prominence of Zeke's face.

"Sod off, you freak," she murmured into her pillow. But those eyes could not be extinguished and soon her own hands became his until she was convinced his weight lay upon her, pressing down and further inside her. The release was exquisite, lasting much longer than she'd ever felt before; as if finally relinquishing control. Sophie took pleasure from this thought before it all gradually subsided.

For the next few nights Sophie left the shower window and her bedroom curtains wide open, imagining him watching her.

That Sunday in the afternoon as she lolled on the sofa, her phone vibrated its chiming ring-tone to an unknown number. Sophie took the call but said nothing.

"Hello? Sophie?" It was definitely him. "Hiya Sophe. I wanted to apologise for the other day…"

"How did you get my number?"

"You know what we were talking about the other day? His name's Gareth isn't it? Your cousin I mean. He really hurt you didn't he? You can talk to me, you know – I really do care…"

Sophie pressed the 'end call' button and contacted her service provider to block his number.

When he hadn't called or appeared for a whole week, Sophie hoped he'd given up on her. She changed her daily routines, trying out new shops and cafes, then decided to take a week off work to go and visit her mum. Gina sorely missed Joshua, her late husband, but got on well with her life, and was especially involved in the local church on the coffee rota and regularly visiting pensioners in the nearby old people's home.

Sophie liked seeing her mum. She'd only left home four years before but still craved her Sunday roasts and home-baked bread. Their close relationship remained based on mutual respect and fondness; although in reality they shared very little in common. It felt less like home without Dad there.

"Hallo, poppet." Gina warmly embraced her daughter. "Look who's come to see us." Sophie knew her mum was talking to Gypsy the ginger cat, usually found slinking around his mistress' feet. Mum and daughter squeezed each other then stepped back still holding hands. Gina led the way in to the neat bungalow through its side door arched with honeysuckle.

They enjoyed each other's company weeding the flower beds, making bread and then strolling through meadows to spot the early orchids.

"The simple life is by far the best one," Sophie mused as they ambled hand in hand.

"Cheeky. Who are you calling simple?" Gina giggled like a teenager.

"We make life too complicated sometimes. Don't you think?"

"Life is very complicated, unfortunately. Just when you think things are going well, tragedy occurs."

Sophie remained silent as a mark of respect. They both knew what she meant.

"And then things happen to bring joy into our lives." Gina tightened her grip. "Not sure what I'd do without you, my darling."

"Don't be daft," Sophie scolded gently. "All I do is whinge and bring you my problems."

"Nonsense, I'm your mother and I'm always here for you."

Sophie let go of Gina's hand and stooped over a pink pyramid-shaped orchid. Using her phone she took a photo for later identification.

"You're always here to sort out my latest relationship fiasco."

"Relationships are the hardest thing, dear, and you'll always get a lot of unwanted attention because you inherited my devastating beauty and sexy figure."

Sophie took hold of her hand again.

"Bet you've loads of men on the go, eh?" Sophie teased. "Frustrated husbands, vicars and postmen."

"You don't know the half of it, my dear. And anyway, you're just jealous."

Gina was sensitive enough not to interrogate her daughter about her love-life, yet the subject always hung there like a perennial question mark. Sophie decided not to tell about Zeke. She didn't want to worry her mum – or describe her darkest desires.

With her rubber-gloved hands in the washing up bowl after tea, Gina took her daughter by surprise.

"There's someone I'd like you to meet, Sophie."

"A shrink?" Sophie wrapped up a soapy plate in the damp tea towel.

"Goodness, no. Nothing like that." Gina refused to look up from her washing up. "No, an old school friend of yours. A lovely lad, just moved back into the area and started coming to church. He told me he was in your English class."

"What's his name?"

"Dan."

"Oh, there may have been a Dan – can't remember now."

"Perhaps he was one of the nice quiet ones. You know someone with qualifications and prospects as opposed to the wasters you hung around with."

"Mother!" Sophie voiced her shock.

"Well, it needs to be said. I'm sure you're through that phase now. You're probably thinking more long-term these days."

"You're match-making, you little minx." Sophie's tone changed to exasperation. "You've already marked this Dan down as a prospective husband, haven't you? And how many children will I have in this grand plan of yours?" She hated the sound of Dan already: a church-boy; probably an accountant or something; and even worse – he met with her mother's full approval.

"Don't get angry with me. I'm looking after your best interests," Gina pouted.

"Yours more likely," Sophie added quickly. "Oh God, how embarrassing. My life is so sad I need my mum to chat up my boyfriends for me."

"Oh for goodness sake. I thought you might like to catch up with an old friend."

"Not really…"

"So I took the liberty of inviting him over this evening." Gina watched the dish water circle down the drain then tugged her apron over her head.

"You did what?" Sophie felt like smashing the plate she held. "When's he coming?"

"Any minute now."

"Bloody hell, Mum. Didn't you think to consult me first?"

"But he's such a lovely young man and he's been a great help to me doing gardening and odd jobs around the house. You know how it's been without your Dad."

"But you've got me to come and help," Sophie said, feeling hurt.

"You're so busy, darling, and Dan is very practical and helpful. Not that you're not helpful – that's not what I'm saying…"

"Okay, Mum, stop digging your hole. Sounds more to me like you have a young admirer. A toy-boy, eh?" Sophie prodded Gina on the shoulder.

Just then the doorbell rang.

"He's always asking after you, Sophie." Gina went to the front door whilst Sophie spied through the gap in the kitchen door.

Her worst fear was confirmed.

"Hello, Gina." Zeke stepped into the hallway and kissed Gina on the cheek.

"Can I get you a cup of tea, Dan?" Gina gestured for him to sit down in the living room. "I know Sophie will be pleased to catch up with you."

Sophie stood her ground in the kitchen.

"Are you coming in, dear? Come and see if you recognise him. You've got lots to chat about."

"Oh, I know him alright and we've got plenty to chat about."

"Shall I leave you to it?" Gina smiled, pleased with herself.

"No Mum," Sophie said in a grave tone. "I'd very much like you to come and listen to what I have to say to him."

Gina picked up the tension as her expression became one of concern.

"Is there something wrong?"

"Come with me and you can decide."

They walked together to confront him.

"Who sent you then?" Sophie forced herself not to move or blink.

"What do you mean, Sophe?"

"Is this some kind of sick joke? Did Gareth put you up to this? He's sent you to come and laugh at me – to mess around with my head. That was always his style."

"Gareth?" Gina interrupted, confused. "What, you mean our Charlie's Gareth? What's it got to do with him? What exactly is going on here?"

Sophie stared ahead and tried not to show she was shaking.

"Perhaps Dan here – or Zeke as he's sometimes known – would like to explain to you why he's been stalking and spying on me."

Zeke remained sat down, rubbing the corner of his left eye with his index finger. Then he looked calmly at both ladies and bit his bottom lip.

"I was scared I'd lost you."

Sophie felt the now familiar annoyance returning. "But there's nothing going on between us. He came up to me in the street and declared his undying love whilst saying things he could never have known. It is Gareth isn't it who sent you?"

"What has your cousin got to do with this?" Gina asked.

"We had an affair, Mum. We were lovers."

"What, you and Gareth? I didn't know anything about that."

"No, Mum." Sophie kept looking forward. "This man has been pretending to know you just to get to me. You've been used. I'm afraid he's not a good little church boy, but a sad pervert who ought to be locked up."

He stood up, raising both hands with fingers spread pleadingly.

"Please listen. I'm not a pervert or stalker. I haven't been sent by anyone. I've never met this Gareth but if I did I'd punch his lights out. Please can we all sit down. I'm not here to threaten anybody." Gina sat down first followed by Sophie then Zeke. "Gina, I admit I did use you but not for anything like that. I needed to see Sophie. I have something to tell you I just know you'll never believe, but I want to say it to both of you. I'm in love with Sophie and I need you to give me a chance to explain myself without any interruptions or accusations. I will tell you the truth but I'm scared you'll think me a raving lunatic. I've already begun to give you evidence that I know you, Sophie, and believe me I do." He took a breath and sat forward in his chair. "Gina, I want you to believe that I really like you – I always have. I felt terrible using you, but glad to be able to help out. I know you want what's best for your daughter and believe me, nobody will ever love her more than I do. Will you give me one last chance?"

"Don't listen, Mum."

Gina nodded for him to continue and indicated with her eyes for Sophie to sit down.

"My real name is Zeke. I'm sorry I lied, Gina, but I might never have got to see Sophie again."

"I don't understand how you know these things about me." Sophie narrowed her eyes and pursed her lips expectantly.

Zeke gave a pained look. "I had hoped to impress you but I miscalculated and I can see now why you don't trust me." He scratched behind his ear like a mischievous puppy. "I need to convince you of the truth before I tell you what I have to say."

"But anyone can play parlour tricks. You've obviously found some confidential information on me and are trying to use it to your own advantage." Sophie wanted answers.

"I could always call the police," Gina added helpfully. "They could help sort this all out."

"No, I promise that won't be necessary, Gina. I'm not dangerous. Possibly an idiot..."

"Ain't that the truth," Sophie muttered audibly.

"If I tell you what I know about Josh – I mean your Dad – would that convince you?"

"Convince us of what?" Gina shuffled in her seat.

"You're treading on dangerous ground here, mister," Sophie's voice turned to a snarl.

"I know," Zeke conceded. "I know how important he was ... is to you, Sophie. I know how close you were to him; both of you. He kept the family together with his charm and wit. When you had your breakdown, Gina, Josh was the one who kept everyone together. He nursed you through terrible times and even when you were at the lowest point of your depression, when you couldn't face your own family and wanted to end it all, Josh was there for you. He managed to hide all this from you, Sophie. In fact you weren't fully aware of your Mum's illness until you were about sixteen because your dad covered it over with his own brand of humour, fun and charisma. He was the man on the moon and you were the moonflower fairy who fell in love with him. That was your favourite game, Sophie."

He looked at the two women who held each other in an intimate embrace, both staring beyond him with tears on their cheeks.

"He pretty much brought you up single-handed," Gina admitted. "He was a truly great man." She paused and took a deep breath. "Then when I had my affair with Charlie, his own brother, he was so understanding. He forgave me and told me he would always love me no matter what I did."

156

"You don't need to do this, mum."

"Yes I do. Josh even blamed himself and he never criticised Charlie, either. Pretended he never knew."

Zeke watched them and sat back silently to let them work it out together.

Sophie felt compelled to confess her sins. "I guess my affair with Gareth was some sort of weird reaction to Dad's death. Not sure if it was anger or revenge. God knows what a psychiatrist would make of it. Dread to think."

"He was taken so cruelly, wasn't he? It was so sudden." Gina realised it was the first time she'd really spoken to her daughter about it.

Overcome with emotion, Sophie sobbed in her mother's arms. Once calm, she turned to Gina and held her face in her hands.

"One good thing came from it, though."

Gina looked puzzled. "What do you mean love?"

"With Dad gone I learnt to love you. For the first time."

Sophie and Gina held each other tightly in a wonderful eternity of silence.

"Okay then, Zeke," Sophie said in a shaky voice. "Tell us how you know this stuff before we get the police to come and lock you away."

Taking a deep breath, Zeke looked up to the ceiling for inspiration.

"Here goes then. I went out with you, Sophe, for over three years and when we split up my world fell apart. You were right to end things with me because I didn't treat you properly."

"Hang on. When you say you went out with me, how come I don't remember? I think I'd recall being with you for three years."

"I will go out with you, Sophe – in your future."

"Honestly, this is such bullshit. Why are we sitting here listening to someone who is clearly unhinged?"

"Your future is my past."

Gina stroked Gypsy who had curled up on her lap. "Are you trying to tell us in all seriousness that you are some kind of time-traveller?"

"I know, it's bizarre," Zeke nodded, his eyes becoming hopeful. "But I somehow went back in time. I arrived about five years back in my own past."

Standing up again, Sophie gave an exasperated sigh. "I think you should leave."

"Have you ever wished you could go back and improve a part of your life?" Zeke continued undeterred. "I knew I had got a part of my life wrong and I begged and prayed to any power listening to let me go back and try again."

"Mum," Sophie pleaded with exasperation, "are you going to let this weirdo carry on. He is clearly deranged and needs medical help."

"I want to hear what he has to say," Gina replied firmly. "We all have things we regret and feel guilty about."

"I was a complete bastard. But it wasn't until I hurt Sophie and left her that I discovered what I'd lost. Losing you made me realise how selfish I am and how much I needed you. You see, Sophe, you complete me. You give me a reason – a purpose…"

"This is such crap," Sophie said, scornfully.

Zeke's expression remained neutral as he considered his next words.

"You're my night, my day, my past, my present and hopefully, my future."

After an elongated beat, Sophie found her next line of reasoning.

"You just told me you were – or will be – a bastard to me." She felt pleased to be thinking lucidly. "So why should I go out with someone who's going to hurt me?"

"I won't."

"How can you be so sure? Can you change the future?"

"No, but it seems I can change the past."

"For you it's the past – or so you say. How can you change the past when it's already happened?"

"But it hasn't happened to you yet."

"You think I'm just going to walk in to an accident waiting to happen?"

"I believe I've been given the gift of a second chance."

"Lucky you."

"Yes, exactly. You've no idea the hell I've been through, but I came out the other side. I now know what love is and it was you who taught me. For some weird reason I'll probably never understand I have the chance to try again – to improve on things. It's like some kind of redemption. Maybe love does control the universe and this is the miracle in our lifetime. We need to grab hold of it, Sophie. I've learned … I'm a better person. I love you. I want to know everything about you – make you happy and fulfilled. I'll be there through the good and bad times, to comfort and support you. To make you laugh. I want us to share memories which will see us through our twilight years. We can have a family – I know you want children – so do I. I know you'd call your daughter Adela and your son Joshua, after your dad. God, there are so many things to talk about but I know if I say everything I'll probably scare you off again."

He stopped for a reaction but received none.

"Please believe me. I'm in love with you, Sophe. I am willing to commit my whole life and self to you. We're part of each other. I know I've pushed you too hard. I'm really sorry. I got it wrong. I panicked."

"It's all so much too quickly," Sophie said feeling her self soften.

"We have plenty of time," Zeke shuffled awkwardly in a way now familiar to her. "The rest of our lives to get to know each other."

"I feel at a slight disadvantage, I must admit," Sophie replied with a frown.

"We can both start again from the beginning."

"It seems like such a big risk."

"Isn't love always a risk?"

Gina, still silently stroked the purring Gypsy, became aware of Sophie looking to her for help.

"Young man. You are either the greatest con-man in the universe – if so I congratulate you on your skills of deception – or something bloody weird is going on."

"Exactly," Zeke remarked. "I don't understand it either."

Sophie's mind clouded up again.

"So how did we meet? Or do we meet? Did you stop me in the street then too and read my palm?"

"No. I got you drunk and took advantage of you." Zeke looked down. "You were going out with my mate, or at least, he was sleeping with you. He said unkind things about you and was seeing other girls, so I saw my chance. I pretended to console you one evening in a bar after I'd told you what he was up to, got you drunk and took you home. I'm ashamed of my actions but I want to be honest with you. Good thing is, it hasn't happened to you yet – not in your reality. I wanted to spare you from him … and from the old me."

"And have me all to yourself."

"What's so bad about that? You see, I didn't appreciate you enough. We started to make a go of it but I took you for granted and you started talking about commitment so I played the game for a while, but like most guys I got scared and went off with another girl. You found out and dumped me – quite rightly. Then I realised what a fuckin' arsehole I was – excuse me Gina."

With a simple hand gesture befitting the Queen of Sheba, Gina excused him.

"I promise not to take advantage of you now or to take you for granted. I'll respect your wishes and we can do things together as partners – equals."

"This sounds almost too good to be true." Sophie remained defensive. But then Gina became suddenly animated.

"On the other hand, dear, opportunities like this are rare. If he's genuine it's worth a risk, I say. I agree with him that life's a gamble."

Zeke stood up.

"I could tell you all over again, Sophe, how much I love you – and I will – every day. I'm offering you something wonderful and exciting. If you tell me to go then I promise to respect you and you'll never hear from me again. You have my word."

After a long silence he stood up and put his hand in his pocket to check for his car keys.

"I think I should leave you to it. Thanks Gina. Please forgive me my deception and lies. I can only hope you'll understand why I did it." He turned to Sophie with pursed lips. "I think we'll say the ball's in your court."

As he shuffled to the doorway, Gina nudged Sophie.

"Tell him to sit down you idiot. God, do I have to do everything for you? You're a grown woman for goodness sake, start acting like one and get a grip on your life."

Zeke stopped without looking round as Sophie rose to her feet and moved towards him. She took hold of his hand and gently tugged him back in to the room.

"Sit down you big lug. Mum's got another bottle of wine to open, haven't you?"

With a sudden realisation Gina jumped up.

"Yes. I'll go and get it right now. Please Zeke, you will stay won't you?"

With a daft grin Zeke looked at the woman he loved.

"I will if Sophie wants me to."

Sophie placed her hand inside his larger one and led him next to her on the couch.

"I want you to tell me everything. We might need more than one bottle, Mum. I have a feeling this could be quite a long night."

WRITER'S BLOCK

To have married one exploding wife was unfortunate, but to have married two was just getting silly. I had starting to take it personally.

The first had combusted spontaneously and photographs of her charred remains are available now in the public domain thanks to various bizarre websites and the inevitable article in 'The Fortean Times'. The photo is of a pile of ash on the burnt carpet of my front room, lying next to the remains of a shoe. I've lost count of the number of detectives, psychic investigators and journalists that interrogated me. I was variously accused of murder, arson, faking the whole spectacle and of being a self-publicist.

It had been a bad year. I was caught up in a media feeding frenzy during which I was offered unseemly amounts of money for my story, which, of course, I refused. I still remember Jean fondly as she was the first woman I ever loved and after all had promised to remain faithful to her 'for better, for worse'; and it couldn't get much worse than this.

I never expected to find a new lover and had committed myself to the rigours of bachelorhood, when Trudy crowbarred her way into my secluded existence. Stunned by her insistence and passion, she proposed to me and we quickly got married. It was about a year later when I turned on the news to hear that a terrorist attack had gone wrong in London: a suicide bomber had only managed to kill herself. Yes, Trudy was in fact an international terrorist wanted for mass-murder, who had married me only for a green card and working visa. I was charged with conspiring to abet a known terrorist organisation and imprisoned for eight months.

So there you have it – two exploding wives and when I was finally released I went back home an ex-con and a bachelor. As my life became secluded, tedious and empty with the long hours of winter stretching ahead of me, I decided to fulfil an old ambition of mine that had been incubating in my mind as I lay in prison. As a middle-aged, single man with no dependants I became what I'd always wanted to be: a writer.

My first project was to work on my great novel. It was to be revolutionary: breaking all conventions and starting a whole new literary impulse to fulfil the dying promise of postmodernism. Being unconventional and wanting to be remembered as a maverick, I decided not to devise an outline of the story, but to let it evolve and develop with its own life and energy. I saw the plot as a spirit world where characters would be animated into existence taking on their own personalities. It would just be a matter of jotting down what happened as it flashed into my endlessly fertile imagination.

I purchased a laptop and as I explored its technological wonders I found it had free access to the internet and during the first month I spent about fourteen hours a day doing essential research, continually amazed by the variety of stuff available to anybody with the simple press of a few buttons. It was a treasure trove.

It was a drug! By the time I realised that I needed help with my obsession the spring was announcing itself: birds sang, bluebells brought colour to my unweeded garden and I knew something had to be done. I deleted the Internet server from my computer and disabled the phone connection in my study so that the modem became obsolete. That took away the temptation and gave me the chance to do what I really wanted to do: write.

I berated myself for wasting my talent. The sooner the world literally took me into their hands and held me gently as I made them laugh and weep, the sooner my true genius would be recognised. How I liked to imagine my readers as my multifarious lovers: they would caress me and allow me to enter them as we shared private secrets and fantasies. There is something special about the relationship between writer and reader. Thus far I had only been at the receiving end, but now I could feel the power, which was surely mine, as my books would titillate, tease, astound and even manipulate, until I was their master and they worshipped the very pages wherein my thoughts, passions and id were to be laid out before them to inspect with their hungry, curious fingers and minds – my people reaching out for me to feed them until they were sated, nay glutted upon the nourishment of my words, my truth, my very self.

After three weeks I had thirty splendid pages that described the front of the house where my protagonist abided. I employed seventeen words to portray the various greens of the ivy that cascaded down the edifice and then explored the changing textures, smells and moods that occur through the various seasons.

Writing with a fever pitch, I continued to complete nearly ten pages a day, until I had over two hundred pages of fluent, poetic narrative and sparkling wordplay that fizzed with similes, personification, pathetic fallacy, alliteration, onomatopoeia, punning, classical allusion, kenning, tragic irony, portmanteau neologisms and, of course, zeugma.

The house stood as the central image and motif: a metaphor for life itself – dissipating and yet all-sustaining. I was certain this had never been done before. I read and reread my creation, the fruit of my own fecund loins. This was what made me realise with a haunting jolt that this was my true calling. I had the gift to write flawless work and at last my talent was to be shared with the world. Not one single word did I change or rewrite: here it was – perfection.

Then one night, I awoke – perhaps by divine intervention – when it occurred to me that something was missing from my manuscript. How could I have been so blind? I rushed naked to my study and clasping my magnum opus in trembling hands I let my frantic, fumbling, fervent fingers flick furiously through the pages, whilst my facial orbs drank in the inky symbols that shimmered on the parchment. Then it hit me – my novel had no characters!

It was true that there were no discernible characters, only the house that had become an extended metonymy for the people who inhabited it. No actual plot existed; and yet the slow erosion and collapse of a building over seven hundred years was a fascinating story in itself, especially as an allegory for the human condition. The more I thought about it, the angrier I became. Who says all novels must have characters and plots? Why should all fiction have to fit into the stifling limitations of dull, passé genres? Why should I have to stick to boring old conventions, just because the ruling academic classes tell us that this is the format of all fiction and that any deviation from the norm is unacceptable? This kind of hegemonic control made me seethe. My novel may not fit into the canon put together by these shortsighted snobs, but to be an originator you had to think outside the box and go against the flow.

I knew by instinct that the manuscript was a work of genius and I bundled it up into a parcel, the package throbbing in my excited, sweating palms as I sent it off to the world's biggest publishing company. Literary history was about to be made.

It came back two days later, clearly unread, with a terse, general rejection note. Ha! One day when I'm famous I'll make them pay dearly for this.

After that first rejection I just sent multiple submissions to every single publisher in the country: let them squabble over me – why should I have to hang around for them to get themselves sorted? For the next three weeks I got to know my postman well, except that he put in a complaint and refused to deliver any more parcels, forcing me to go down to the local depot and collect the last forty-three myself.

Tweaking. I finally and humbly accepted that that was what it needed: a little bit of editing here and there – although it was nigh on impossible to see how it could be improved. I sat down and planned my time carefully. I would work in sittings of four hours, with half hour breaks between. I allowed myself eleven hours sleep before rising at eight to eat breakfast before the first session.

By now it was summer and test match cricket was shown on television amidst the irresistible lure of soaps, quiz shows and films. By the end of August, even though I watched with the laptop on my lap, I realised I had not written a single word – but these things should not be rushed, and anyway I could justify watching films, as doing so was surely preparation for my work as a writer, as the ideas in my mind were slowly brewing and being unconsciously developed.

It was at this point when I faced a new setback.

Walking home from the shops one late summer's morning it began to rain. I let myself in and, a little soggy, allowed myself to dry and sleep on the sofa – perchance to dream. I awoke about midnight in a fervour of inspiration. The ideas were flowing like a torrent and I rushed to grasp my laptop ere the blossoms of my mind should fall and atrophy. But the laptop was gone! Some jealous thief who resented my talent had stolen my masterpiece that was on its hard disc.

After a bout of panic and a painful asthma attack, I phoned the police and told them of my break-in. Angry when they only sent round a mere constable, I tried to convince him of the importance of my work. He asked how they had entered my abode and I scornfully told him that I should not be doing his job for him. The policeman examined all the windows and front door, before stepping out into my back garden where I had been sat that morning. There on the muddy lawn lay the laptop, still open, but now dirty and obviously unusable. I tried to convince him that some envious rival had destroyed my life's work, but he sneered and called me startling names, suggesting I had left it out in the rain whereupon it had exploded. Threatening to report him to his superiors, I explained that as an artist whose mind transcended the mundane, how was I supposed to remember such trivial, practical things?

The laptop was indeed beyond repair and I couldn't afford another one, so that afternoon I wrote to my insurers who eventually replied politely explaining that because it was my fault coupled with an act of God they could make no payments and that as my excess was greater than the loss anyway then it seemed a pointless claim to make. I took this blow on the chin and tried to accentuate the positive. Once I received my first advance and royalty cheque I would purchase the best computer money could buy.

I still had one manuscript left but for now I had no word processor and had kept no copies of the corroded files, so no amendments could be made. Anyway, what the hell do publishers know? They're just accountants with no artistic sensibilities. What I really needed was an agent who would recognise my raw talents for what they were, who could then guide and shape my writing for the benefit of future generations. I imagined myself giving lectures at festivals and agreeing to doctoral theses from zealous students desperate to analyse my 'oeuvre'.

I won't bore you with an account of the response from every single one of these Neolithic philistines. It was clear to me that I was ahead of my time – misunderstood by these vulgar savages who were dictated by mere 'lowest common denominator' commercialism. My work was not for popular mass consumption anyway – it was literary and artistic. Perhaps the originality of my work overwhelmed them.

Finally, there was one literary agent left who hadn't seen my work: an agency had just opened in London who was calling for new clients in the national press. The now slightly yellow, curling manuscript was duly despatched and I waited with tremulous excitement. I couldn't sleep or eat. I bit my nails to the quick and insisted on sleeping on the doormat, under the letterbox. After a month I became emaciated and feverish. Hair began to fall out in clumps and I slurred my words. Whenever the postman arrived I sat on my haunches and growled. I tried to keep a tally of the days that passed, scratching marks on the wallpaper; and on the one hundred and ninety ninth day, my self addressed parcel finally arrived. The postman was wary of me as I nipped at his ankles, but he threw down the brown package and ran for his life.

Lackaday! Woe is me! Rejection is the bitterest pill to swallow. I threw the manuscript on the floor with disgust and screamed a banshee howl of hatred and outrage. This was it! It was me against the world! But I had little strength left and certainly no more tears. Even my attempt at suicide lacked the necessary energy.

So I stared for days at my manuscript, getting cramp and tremors. Then in sheer desperation, I slowly and carefully rolled up the discarded manuscript, lit the end and smoked it. With each inhalation I could feel the tension diminish and my mind clear; so lucid and full of shapes and colours. As I relaxed into a delirium, my eyes began to close and my mind's eye flickered like the beginning of a movie…

At last, I was inspired – I could see it all like a vision that had captured my soul. I had my own story to tell: about a man with two exploding wives. I had to grab a pen to write it all down immediately whilst it was fresh in the mind and the sensual energy of it still haunted my whole being … or at least after I'd watched that film that was about to start on telly …

www.ingramcontent.com/pod-product-compliance
Lightning Source LLC
Chambersburg PA
CBHW061450210726
48287CB00007B/2440